Greyson's gaze grew intent. "Is that how you repay your debts?"

"I didn't say that," Charlotte said evenly—never mind the erratic beating of her heart. "I'm simply giving you the opportunity to reconsider your options. Fictional fiancées are more trouble than they're worth. Trust me on this—I'm doing you a favor by pointing it out."

"You're very kind," he said smoothly. "I propose an experiment. Something that lets me decide if bringing you along to meet the family is going to work." He came closer then. Close enough for her to feel the heat in that big lean body of his. Close enough for her to catch the scent of him. Tantalizingly male, undeniably appealing. And then there was his mouth. Such a tempting mouth.

"Kiss me," he murmured, and her eyes flew to his.

"Excuse me?"

"That's the experiment," he said. "If there's no chemistry we're square. Finished." His lips moved closer. "Through." Greyson's lips brushed hers, and Charlotte drew a ragged breath. "No family BBQ." And then his lips were on hers, warm and coaxing, not demanding—not yet.

Teasing, those lips of his.

Practiced, the hand that came up to cradle her skull and position her for deeper invasion, only he didn't invade—not yet.

Torture first.

And then he closed his eyes, slid his mouth over hers and simply took.

Accidentally educated in the sciences, **KELLY HUNTER** has always had a weakness for fairy tales, fantasy worlds and losing herself in a good book. Husband…yes. Children…two boys. Cooking and cleaning…sigh. Sports… no, not really—in spite of the best efforts of her family. Gardening…yes. Roses, of course. Kelly was born in Australia and has traveled extensively. Although she enjoys living and working in different parts of the world, she still calls Australia home.

Kelly's novels *Sleeping Partner* and *Revealed: A Prince and a Pregnancy* were both finalists for a Romance Writers of America RITA® Award, in the Best Contemporary Series Romance category.

Visit Kelly online at www.kellyhunter.net.

WITH THIS FLING...

KELLY HUNTER

~P.S. I'M PREGNANT! ~

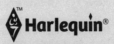

TORONTO NEW YORK LONDON
AMSTERDAM PARIS SYDNEY HAMBURG
STOCKHOLM ATHENS TOKYO MILAN MADRID
PRAGUE WARSAW BUDAPEST AUCKLAND

Recycling programs
for this product may
not exist in your area.

ISBN-13: 978-0-373-52819-6

WITH THIS FLING…

First North American Publication 2011

Copyright © 2011 by Kelly Hunter

www.eHarlequin.com

Printed in U.S.A.

WITH THIS
FLING...

If wishes were fishes, beggars would fly

PROLOGUE

THERE was a lot to be said for fictional fiancés, decided
Charlotte Greenstone as she settled into the saggy vinyl
hospital chair for yet another night-time vigil by her dying
godmother's side. The room had seen decades of sickness
and death but the elderly Aurora refused entry to gloom
and opted instead to remember a life well lived and specu-
late quite outrageously on what might come after death.

Ashes seemed inevitable given that Aurora wanted to be
cremated, but, if not dust, Aurora pondered the layout of
heaven, the hierarchy within it, and how long the waiting
list for reincarnation as a house cat might be.

This night, unfortunately, wasn't shaping up to be one
of Aurora's better nights. Tonight Aurora was morphined-
up and fretful, her main concern being that once she was
gone Charlotte would have no one. Not nothing—for when
it came to worldly possessions Charlotte had more than
enough for any one person. But when it came to family and
a sense of belonging…when it came down to the number of
people Charlotte could turn to for comfort and company…
Aurora's concerns weren't entirely unfounded. Hence the
invention of Charlotte's tailor-made handy-dandy fictional
fiancé. A wonderfully useful man if ever there was one.

Dashing.

Deliciously honourable.

Modest yet supremely accomplished.

And, last but not least, absent.

Once the awkwardness of the initial deception had passed, the fictional fiancé had provided endless hours of bedside entertainment. More to the point, his presence— so to speak—had provided valuable reassurance to a godmother who needed it that Charlotte would be loved. That she wouldn't be lonely. Not with the likes of Thaddeus Jeremiah Gilbert Tyler around.

Not that anyone actually called the man Thaddeus to his face, oh, no. His research colleagues called him Tyler, and they uttered the name respectfully given his status as an independently wealthy globetrotting botanist, humanitarian, eco warrior, and citizen of Australia. His mother called him TJ. Always had, always would. Thaddeus Jeremiah Gilbert's father called him son, and bore a startling resemblance to Sean Connery. The adventurous Mr Tyler had no siblings—easier just to make him like Charlotte in that regard.

Charlotte called him Gil and laced the word with affection and desire, and Aurora believed.

Gil was in Papua New Guinea, somewhere up the Sepik River where phones were few and contact with the outside world was practically non-existent. Charlotte had managed to get a message through to him though…finally…and he'd sent a tribesman back to Moresby with a message for her. He hoped to be there soon, for he'd missed Charlotte most desperately and never wanted to be parted from her again. He wanted to meet Aurora, for he'd heard so much about her: accomplished businesswoman, artefact collector, godmother and all round good fairy; he wanted to meet the woman who'd raised his beloved Charlotte.

Aurora wanted to meet *him*.

The wonderfully eccentric Aurora Herschoval being

the closest thing to family Charlotte had ever had, for her parents were long dead, over twenty years dead now, and little more than a glamorous memory.

The cancer-ridden and increasingly morphine-medicated Aurora had a tendency to confuse Gil with Charlotte's father. Easy enough to do, Charlotte supposed, seeing as she'd modelled the man on the bits of her father she remembered.

Gil, aka TJ, aka Thaddeus Jeremiah Gilbert Tyler, in other words her fictional fiancé, also paid homage to Indiana Jones—complete with hat; Captain Kirk—probably best not to try and figure out why; and a swaggering Caribbean pirate or two—minus the hygiene issues. Yes, indeed, Charlotte's fiancé was quite a man.

She'd miss him dreadfully when he was gone. His zest for life and new experiences. His tenderness and his wit. His company, as daft as that sounded, for he *had* kept her company these long anxious nights. He'd helped her keep the tears at bay and given her the strength to face what was coming.

Aurora passed away right on time. Two months from the discovery of the cancer to the finish, just as the good doctor had predicted.

This time, the thought of Gilbert did not hold Charlotte's tears at bay. She wept with relief that Aurora's pain had finally ceased. She wept with grief for the loss of a mother and friend.

She just wept.

Gilbert didn't make it home to Australia in time to meet Aurora—an unforgivable act of negligence as far as Charlotte was concerned. Poetic justice came swiftly.

Gilbert, in his haste to return to her, had ventured into territory he had no business venturing into. Once there, the reckless—yet noble—fool had tried to prevent the kidnapping of tribal daughters by a renegade hunting party, so it was said. Authorities had little hope of recovering his remains. The words *'long pig'* had been whispered.

It was a double blow, his demise coming so soon after Aurora's, and in the wee small hours of the night Charlotte mourned for him.

She really did.

CHAPTER ONE

'CHARLOTTE, what are you doing here?' Professor Harold Mead's panicked expression didn't quite fit his soothing fatherly tone. Then again, a lot of things about her boss didn't quite fit. Like his version of Ancient Egyptian history as opposed to everyone else's, for example. Or his idea of a regular working week, which was somewhere in the vicinity of seventy hours as opposed to, say, the fifty everyone else put in.

Granted, it was seven-thirty on a Monday morning and she didn't usually start work quite this early, but still…she *did* have every right to be here. 'Charlotte?' he repeated.

'Working?' she offered helpfully. 'At least, that's the plan. Is there something wrong with the plan?'

'No, but we were hardly expecting you in today. We thought you might take a few days to come to terms with your loss, what with your godmother's funeral yesterday.' Which he'd attended. Which had been nice of him, seeing as he hadn't known Aurora well at all.

'It was a good funeral,' she said softly. 'A celebration of a life well lived. That's what I think. That's what I know. And thank you for attending.'

'You're welcome,' said the Mead. 'And if you do need to take a few days' leave…'

'No,' said Charlotte hastily. 'Please. No leave. I'm fine.' She tried on a smile, and saw from the deepening concern in the Mead's eyes that he'd seen it for the falsehood it was. 'Really. I'm ready to work. I think I have a lead on what the pottery fragments coming out of the Loess site might be.'

'It can wait,' said the Mead. 'Or you could pass that work on to someone else. Dr Carlysle, perhaps? Seeing as he's on site? Dr Steadfellow values him quite highly.'

'I'm sure he does.' Steadfellow's reports had been full of the man. 'But I'd rather not.' The Loess site had been one of her finds. Hers and Aurora's. She'd *given* Steadfellow that site—co-ordinates, preliminary work, everything—on condition that she took part in the analysis. Alas, the good Dr Steadfellow seemed to be in danger of forgetting their arrangement now that the highly valued Dr Carlysle had joined the team. 'Harold, I know Dr Steadfellow and Dr Carlysle feel they can take it from here. I know they're eminently qualified to do so but that's not the point. I feel like I'm being sidelined and that wasn't the arrangement.'

'Charlotte, be reasonable,' said the Mead soothingly. 'Everyone knows you pulled together the funding for the Loess dig. No one doubts your claim to significant project input, but is this really a good time to be challenging your colleagues? Might they not simply be trying to help you through a difficult personal patch?'

Charlotte heard the words. She wanted to believe in them. Wanted to trust that Steadfellow would honour his word and acknowledge her contribution to the discovery, but in all honesty she just didn't know if he would. Her judgement was shot, these days. Too many sleepless nights. Too much weaving in and out of imaginary realities because it had hurt too much to stay in *this* one. 'I'll talk to

Steadfellow. And Carlysle,' she said quietly. 'We'll sort something out.'

'Excellent.' The Mead beamed. 'I knew you'd be generous about this. You already have more publications than most archaeologists three times your age. A tenured position is just around the corner for you.'

'Even if I'm seen as a pushover?' she asked quietly and Harold had the grace to flush.

'Charlotte,' he said. 'I know your godmother was of great assistance to you when it came to contacts in the archaeology world. I know your family name engenders a great deal of goodwill. God knows, I've *never* seen an archaeologist pull funding from the private sector the way you do. But your godmother's gone now, and a lot of people will be looking to see if your legendary contacts went with her.' He took a breath and fixed her with what he probably thought was a kindly gaze. 'Charlotte, you're a wonderful asset to this department, but if you'll take an old man's advice—and I do hope you will—losing ground on the Loess dig is the least of your problems. You need to think about taking to the field for a while and renewing your contacts in person. You need to think about getting back out on site and heading up your own digs. That's what I'd be doing if I were you and I *really* wanted to get back in the game. Your position then would be unassailable. If that's what you want.'

If that's what you want.

Truth was—Charlotte didn't know *what* she wanted any more, when it came to her work.

And the Mead knew it.

'Charlotte, I know you're not given to discussing your private life with your work colleagues,' the Mead began awkwardly. 'But I heard what happened to your fiancé in PNG. Bad business, that. Terrible.'

'You, ah…heard about that?' Charlotte's heart thumped hard against her chest, and if her smile was a little strained it was only because the situation warranted it. Thaddeus Jeremiah Gilbert Tyler was supposed to have lived only in her mind and Aurora's. No one else's. 'How?'

'One of the palliative care nurses up at the hospital is married to Thomas over in Statistics. He's been keeping us abreast of various…things.'

'Oh.' Charlotte offered up another sickly smile, dimly registering the collision of planet fiction with planet reality but having no idea how to wrest them back apart. Why couldn't she have simply broken her fictitious engagement to her fictitious fiancé in a sane and sensible manner, rather than killing him off? That way the formerly useful Gil could have gone paddling up the Sepik for ever, and she and Harold would not be having this conversation.

'At least with your godmother you were prepared for her death. But with your fiancé, and without the body… Anyway, enough of that. Charlotte, I reiterate—if you need to take some extended leave, please do.'

'I—thank you.' Charlotte's voice shook alarmingly. The Mead took a giant step back, as if downright horrified at the prospect of Charlotte in tears. He wasn't the only one to be horrified by such a notion. *Stop it, Charlotte. Shoulders back. Don't you dare break down. A Greenstone never breaks down. Chin up, Charlie, and smile.* The last was pure Aurora.

Slowly, very slowly, Charlotte collected her composure and offered up what she hoped would pass for a smile. 'Thank you, Harold. I appreciate your concern and your advice, I really do. But right now, I'd really rather work.'

If Charlotte thought her early morning conversation with the Mead had been bad, morning tea in the staffroom was worse. Kind words cut deep when they weren't deserved, and there were a *lot* of kind words for Charlotte this morning on account of her loss.

Loss*es*.

She cut out fast, back to her little corner office, taking her cup of tea with her. Once there she slumped into her chair and stared at her computer screen without really seeing it. Surely things would be better tomorrow? Surely this overwhelming sense of loss on the one hand and guilt on the other would fade? All she had to do was ride out these next few days. Maybe she could resurrect Gil and then dump him? Or have him dump her. Mutually agree to part ways…

'How're you holding up?' said a voice from the doorway. Millie, seeking entry, offering solace. Millie, who deserved better than lies from her.

'So-so.' Charlotte offered up a weak smile. 'Sympathy on account of Aurora's death I can handle. I'm not so sure I can handle any sympathy on account of Gil.'

'It's not so much sympathy as rampant curiosity,' said Millie as she came in and perched her skinny rear on the edge of the table. 'We've been friends and co-workers for, what, almost two years now? Why didn't you *tell* me you were engaged? And why aren't you wearing his ring?'

'It was a fairly loose arrangement,' said Charlotte awkwardly. 'Really loose.'

'How long since you'd seen him?' asked Millie.

'A while. Gil was very independent. Adventurous.' For a moment, Charlotte let herself dream. 'Gil was a law unto himself. Passionate and focused. Energetic. Patient…'

'Stamina?'

'That too.'

'I'm beginning to see the appeal,' said Millie. 'Unless you actually happened to want him around.'

Charlotte snapped out of her Gilfest with a wry smile. 'Well, there was that.'

'Do I sense a shred of relief that you're no longer tied to such an independent adventurer?'

'You might,' murmured Charlotte. This was what she wanted, wasn't it? Millie and everyone else to think that she'd recover quickly from her fiancé's demise? Why on earth, then, should she feel so disloyal to *Gil*?

'Do you have a picture of him?' asked Millie.

'What?'

'A photo. Of your fiancé.'

'Somewhere I do.' The lies, they just kept coming. 'Honestly, Millie. I'm okay. I may have embellished Gil's importance for Aurora's benefit. Just a little.'

'You should dig out a picture,' said Millie gently. 'Put it up. Swear at it if it makes you feel better. Even if he wasn't the marrying kind, even if your engagement was a colossal mistake, you should celebrate the time you spent with him. It's *okay* to feel conflicted about his death, Charlotte. It's okay to get *angry* with him for putting himself in a position to get eaten. It's all part of the grieving process and it's perfectly normal.'

'It's really not,' said Charlotte faintly. Nothing about these last two months had been normal. 'Everything's gone a little bit crazy. Starting with me.'

'That's because prolonged bedside vigils will do that to a person. Which is why you shouldn't be here,' said Millie earnestly. 'Seriously, Charlotte. Why don't you take a few days' leave? Head for the coast. Rent a lighthouse. Refresh your spirit. Allow yourself to grieve.'

Charlotte shook her head, hot tears not far from falling. 'I can't.'

'Why not?'

'Because I need to keep busy.' She gave Millie the truth

of it, and felt marginally better for doing so. 'I need to be around other people, people I know, even if they do think I'm a spoiled archaeology heiress with fading networking skills and no brains.'

'Says who?' said Millie sharply. 'Did the Mead say that to you?' And without waiting for Charlotte's reply, 'Moron.'

'He didn't say that.' Charlotte felt obliged to defend him. 'He was really very kind. He just…'

'Implied it,' said Millie darkly. 'I know how he works.'

'Maybe he didn't imply it,' said Charlotte. 'Maybe I did. Maybe it's just a big day for self doubt.' And loneliness. It was a hell of a day for that. 'Thing is, I need to feel as if I'm part of a community today, and this community is the only one I've got. Does that sound needy?'

'No.' Millie's smile came free and gentle and washed over Charlotte like a balm. 'It sounds like your community needs to lift its game.'

For all her inquisitiveness, Millie Peters had a good heart and for the rest of the day she did everything in her power to ensure that Charlotte had company. Half the archaeology department went to the cinema with them that evening. The following evening Millie and her latest beau, Derek, invited Charlotte to dine with them at a local pub.

Derek was an archaeology student with a builder's licence in his back pocket, a double degree in geology and ancient history, and a blissfully practical outlook for someone bent on becoming a field archaeologist.

They found a small round table over by the window, not too sticky, not too wobbly, and settled in for the duration. Derek bought the first round of drinks and the barman went back to filling his fridges, and the pool players went back to smacking their balls around as lazy jazz played softly through oversized speakers. Not bad. Infinitely better than being at home.

'The crispy pork sounds good,' said Derek, and Millie glared meaningfully at him.

'The crispy pork does *not* sound good,' countered Millie. 'Have the beef. Or the duck. No mistaking duck for anything but duck.' Millie's face disappeared behind her menu. 'Remember what I told you about the *long pig* incident,' she muttered to Derek as quietly as she could, which wasn't nearly quietly enough.

Derek slid Charlotte a lightning glance and promptly disappeared behind his menu too. 'Where's the duck?' he said.

'Halfway down the specials list,' murmured Millie. 'Have it braised.'

'Why not barbecued?' Derek whispered back. 'You're just *assuming* he was barbecued. They could have braised him. They could have *boiled* him.'

'You're right,' muttered Millie. 'Order the vegetable combo.'

At which point Charlotte reached across the table and pulled Millie's menu down past eye level. 'Psst.'

'What?' Millie eyed her warily.

'Millie, let the poor man eat pork. I don't care if he wants it crucified, I promise I won't see it as a metaphor for him eating Gil.'

Derek's menu dipped slowly. Derek's eyes appeared, followed by a nose, very nice cheekbones, and a wide wry smile.

'I knew she was saner than you,' Derek told Millie and barely winced when Millie's menu clipped his shoulder. They were very broad shoulders. Millie might just have to keep this one.

'So what was he like?' asked Derek. 'Your fiancé.'

'He's hard to define, but if I had to sum him up I'd probably go with *useful*,' said Charlotte. Nothing but the truth.

'Useful as in "Honey, could you fix the hot water system?"' asked Millie.

'I'm sure he *could* have fixed the hot water system,' said Charlotte. 'Had it needed fixing.'

'Can't everyone?' countered Derek.

'Sadly, no,' said Charlotte.

'I dare say Gil was modest too,' said Millie, glancing pointedly at Derek.

'What?' said Derek. 'I can be modest.'

'Of course you can,' murmured Charlotte, eyeing Derek's frayed shirt collar and shaggy hair speculatively. 'Gil was a snappy dresser too, in a rustic, ready for anything kind of way.'

'Window dressing,' said Derek. 'It's the body beneath the clothes that counts and don't either of you try and tell me different.'

'Wouldn't dream of it,' said Charlotte. 'But just for your information, that was superb too.'

'Well, it would be,' said Millie. 'What with all that paddling up the river. I bet the man had fabulous upper-body definition.'

'I was a lumberjack once,' said Derek.

'Of course you were,' murmured Millie consolingly.

A youthful waitress stepped up to their table, smile at the ready as she asked them if they were ready to order.

'I'll have the pork,' said Derek. 'But could I have it beaten first?'

'Chef runs it through a tenderiser,' said the waitress. 'You know—one of those old-fashioned washing-machine wringer things with the spikes?'

'Perfect,' said Derek.

'Unlike some things around here,' murmured Millie.

'No man is perfect,' said Derek. 'Especially in the eyes of women. A determined woman can turn even a man's *good* qualities into major flaws of character given time and motive, and half the time the motive is optional. It's just something you do.'

'There's got to be an ex-wife in your past somewhere,' murmured Charlotte. 'C'mon, Derek. Spill.'

'Never.'

'Maybe an overcritical mother,' said Millie.

'I'm an orphan,' said Derek. 'Never knew my parents. Never got adopted. Ugliest baby in the world, according to Sister Ramona.'

'That explains a lot,' murmured Millie. 'Though it doesn't explain how you got to be quite so handsome *now*. In a craggy, hard-living kind of way.'

'Thank you,' said Derek blandly.

'You're welcome.'

They finished ordering their meals. They started in on their drinks.

'Here's to the wonderful Aurora Herschoval,' said Charlotte. 'The best godmother an orphan could have.'

'Hear hear,' said Derek. 'Good for you. And here's to Useful Gil. May he be blessed with more brains in his next life.'

'*Derek!*' said Millie, aghast. 'We can't toast to that.'

'Why not?' said Derek, aiming for an expression of craggy, hard-lived innocence. 'Sweetie, he may have been handy, handsome, modest, and built like Apollo, but let's be honest here…the man got eaten.'

CHAPTER TWO

A WEEK passed, and then another, and Charlotte kept busy. She applied herself diligently, if not wholeheartedly, to her work. She considered the merits of Harold's suggestion to hit the archaeology road again for a while and came to no firm conclusion. She inherited Aurora's wealth and her Double Bay waterfront estate on Sydney Harbour.

And when it came to dead fictional fiancés, she kept right on lying.

Was it too late to tell Millie the truth about Gil? To tell everyone the truth?

The question plagued her. 'When, when, *when*?' her conscience demanded. And, 'Too late, too late, too late,' the devil kept saying smugly. Bad friend to Millie. Too late to tell the Mead that Gil had been nothing more than a figment of her imagination. That time had passed. Her detractors within the archaeology world and the university system would flay her if she did.

'What did I tell you?' they would say smugly to each other. 'I always knew she was too reckless to hold down a position of responsibility, no matter *what* pull her family name has in high places.' Then they'd shake their heads and say what a loss Charlotte's parents had been to archaeology with one breath, and castigate them for being too bold on the other. 'Crazy runs in the family,' they'd say.

'And the godmother was cut from the same cloth. Always chasing rainbows. No wonder poor Charlotte has trouble separating fantasy from reality…'

'*Charlotte!*'

A distant voice, sharp and concerned.

'What?' Charlotte blinked and there was Millie. Tortoiseshell glasses framing earnest hazel eyes set in a heart-shaped face.

'You didn't hear me come in. You didn't hear me calling your name.'

'Sorry,' murmured Charlotte. 'Must've been daydreaming.'

Millie winced. Probably because she thought Charlotte had been spending a little too much time in that state of late.

'What's up?' said Charlotte, determined to forestall any actual complaint about her not entirely firm hold on reality.

Millie hesitated. Millie fidgeted. Millie was not in a good place right now and Charlotte didn't quite know why. Time to ask Millie what was wrong and see if there was any way in which she could help. Good friend, Charlotte. *Good* friend.

'Don't kill me,' said Mille anxiously.

'O-kay,' said Charlotte carefully. Not quite the response she'd been expecting.

'I was only trying to help,' said Millie next.

'And?'

'And I emailed the Research Institute in PNG to see if they had a photo of Gil anywhere that they could send to you. A memento. Something tangible for you to remember him by. I, ah, signed it in your name.'

'And?' said Charlotte, with an impending sense of doom.

'And his secretary wrote back and said she'd see what she could find and was it okay to send everything to your university address. To which I said yes.'

'And?'

'And there's a huge packing box downstairs, addressed to you from PNG. I think it might be Gil's effects.'

Charlotte blinked. 'His...*effects*?'

Millie nodded. 'I swear all I asked for was a photo. I never once implied that you were his next of kin or that you wanted all his stuff. I mean, he does have other family, right? Parents and so forth.'

'Right,' said Charlotte faintly.

'And you know how to contact them, right?'

'Er...right.'

'So, do you want the box up here or in your car? At the moment it's sitting by the stairs on the ground floor.'

Charlotte blinked again. 'I think I need to see it.' Hopefully the trip down two flights of stairs would give her time to *think*.

A dozen flights of stairs would have been better.

All too soon, Charlotte and Millie stood at the bottom of the stairs, staring at a large removalist box with her name and university address on it. A nervous giggle escaped Charlotte. She countered by putting one hand to her mouth and the other hand to her elbow. The Standing Thinker pose.

'So...' said Millie. 'Where do you want it?'

'I'm thinking we take it upstairs for now,' Charlotte muttered finally. 'I may need to send it...on.'

There was no lift in the building.

'I'll get a trolley,' said Millie. 'And Derek.'

'Thanks,' murmured Charlotte, still staring at the box.

* * *

They got the box upstairs and into Charlotte's office eventually. Neither Millie nor Derek seemed of a mind to linger. They fled.

Charlotte tried ignoring the box, at first. That didn't go well.

The compulsion to open the box and find out exactly what the good souls at the PNG Research Institute had seen fit to send her took control. A pair of office scissors later and the flaps on top of the box sprung open. Tentatively, Charlotte folded them back.

The first thing she saw was a man's collared business shirt, the really expensive wash-n-wear kind of dress shirt that didn't need ironing and always looked fabulous. Size: Large. Colour: Ivory. A hat came next, an honest to God, Indiana Jones-style Akubra that looked as if it had been trampled by a herd of elephants and then dragged through a river backwards. Well-worn jeans came next, the kind that had earned their faded knees and ragged hems the old-fashioned way. Then some scuffed leather walking boots and thick socks. No other smalls whatsoever. Commando Indy.

Books came next, an extensive library of botany books and journals. Then came file upon file of research papers in haphazard order. A laptop had been tucked in between them. There was a round wall clock that still worked but told the wrong time. A handful of USB storage devices had been sealed inside an envelope. She unearthed a plastic takeaway container full of the stuff one might find in an office drawer. There were no photos.

The last thing she pulled from the box was a door tag with the name Dr G Tyler printed on it, the lettering no-nonsense black on a white background. A similar contraption graced her own door, and almost every other door in this building.

Charlotte stood back, ran unsteady hands through already wayward curls and surveyed the items strewn around her. She didn't need to be an archaeologist to know what she had here.

Heaven help her, they'd sent her someone's office.

The first thing to do was not panic.

So what if Dr G Tyler was going to be mighty unhappy when he discovered that his research wasn't where he left it? That someone had packed up the contents of his office and shipped it off to…her? Belongings could be returned. Repacked and returned to sender with a brief note of apology for the confusion. Email! His computer would have his email address on it. She could send him an email and let him know that his office was on its way back to him. Of course, said email might not be received by him given that she also had his laptop, but surely the man would be accessing his emails from another computer. He'd be doing that, surely?

Unless the man was dead.

'I did *not* wish you dead,' she muttered. 'Please don't be dead. You'll get your stuff back, I promise. Or if you *do* happen to be dead, I'll make sure this gets to your family.' Only…what if he had a wife? Children! 'I'll explain *everything*,' she said fervently. No way would she allow G Tyler to emerge from this mess with a reputation as a cheating, lying husband with a mistress on the side. 'I *will* come clean.'

I promise.

Greyson Tyler wasn't an unreasonable man. He understood what it took to get scientific research done in remote locations. He tolerated inefficiency in others, applied leeway when needed, and pressure when needed too. He took his time, worked his way calmly and methodically through the red tape associated with such endeavours, and eventually he got his way. He always got his way, eventually, and he always got results.

He'd known he was tempting fate when he'd boxed his office effects up, ready to ship back to Australia, and hadn't personally delivered the box into the hands of the freight carrier. He'd thought twice before leaving that task up to Mariah, the latest in a long line of temporary secretaries. Mariah had potential. She might even make a halfway decent administrative assistant one day. Presuming, of course, that she mastered the art of punctuality.

He'd left her a note with the name of the freight company he wanted to use. He'd left 'Please Send To' details right there on her desk. He'd set his misgivings aside and departed on his final field trip up-river without talking Mariah through the process.

Bad move.

She *had* used the freight company he'd recommended, that was something.

But she swore blue that she'd never seen the mailing address Grey had left for her, so when the email from his fiancée had come in—asking for a photo of him—and said fiancée had also been agreeable to Mariah sending the rest of his things her way, well… Problem solved.

A chain of events that showed initiative and even sounded halfway reasonable, except for one small anomaly.

He didn't have a fiancée.

He did, however, have a shipping address, and a phone call to the University of Sydney's information line gave him a work phone number for his beloved intended.

Charlotte Greenstone was her name, and she was an Associate Professor of Archaeology, no less.

He'd never heard of her.

He was prepared to be considerate, given that there had clearly been a mistake, and that she presumably did have a fiancé in these parts with a similar name to his. He was prepared to give her some leeway when it came to the return of his possessions. And if she *didn't* have his office effects already in her possession, he could warn her that they'd be arriving soon and that he'd be by to collect them.

He'd just completed his final set of measurements. Three years' worth of research all done, which meant he could be out of here.

Not a moment too soon in the opinion of some.

He could be back in Sydney by tomorrow. He could collect his office contents, head for his catamaran moored on the Hawkesbury River just north of Sydney, find a suitably secluded cove to anchor in, and analyse his data from there. His cat was ocean-going and had all the amenities he would need. He'd lived on her before.

He could kiss goodbye lawlessness and brutality and live for a time in a place where one's possessions had a halfway chance of staying *in* one's possession.

Tempting.

He put a call through to Charlotte Greenstone's number and got her answering machine. A warm and surprisingly youthful voice told him to leave a message and she'd get back to him.

It was six-thirty on a Friday afternoon, Sydney time. Chances were that Associate Professor Charlotte had skipped for the weekend already, which meant the soonest he could reasonably expect a call back was Monday morning, her time. By which time he could be *at* her office collecting *his* office. He could be on the catamaran, set up and working, by Monday afternoon.

Aspro Charlotte had left a mobile phone number on her

answering machine for urgent requests. Probably a good idea to check with her before he left PNG that she hadn't turned his belongings around already.

This time when he called he got her in person. Same smooth velvety voice. The kind of voice that slid down a man's spine and reminded him that he hadn't had a woman in a while. He cleared his throat, nonplussed by the notion that he'd responded to the voice of a woman his mother's age. Associate professorship took time.

'Hello?' she said again, and damned if his body didn't respond again and to hell with her advancing years.

'Professor Greenstone, my name's Grey Tyler,' he said hurriedly. '*Dr* Grey Tyler, botanist. I'm calling from PNG.'

Silence at that.

'We're not acquainted but I'm hoping you can help me.' There. He was politeness itself. His mother would be proud. Charlotte Greenstone would be impressed. 'I'm based in Port Moresby, although I spend a lot of time travelling between research sites in the country's interior. I've just returned from such a trip to find that the contents of my office have been shipped to you by mistake.'

'Yes,' she said faintly. 'Yes, Dr Tyler, your belongings arrived today. Did you get my email?'

'Email?' he echoed.

'The one I sent you from your computer in the hope that you were still accessing your emails,' she said. 'Although judging by the several hundred emails that subsequently popped *in* to your inbox, I wasn't all that hopeful.'

'You accessed my *computer*?' What about his password protection? The supposedly unassailable drive he kept his research files on? '*How?*'

'Actually, it was the IT guy who did the accessing,' she confessed. 'He's very good. And we only accessed your emails and we only did that to get your contact details. I tried calling the number in your signature line but you no longer seem to have a functioning phone.'

'Forget the phone, you accessed my *computer*?'

'Dr Tyler, why don't you just tell me where you want your box sent?' Not so mellow now, that gorgeous voice. Impatience had crept in, firing up his own.

'Nowhere. Don't send it anywhere. I'll pick it up on Monday.'

'*What?*' For some reason, Charlotte Greenstone didn't sound overly enamoured of the notion.

'Monday,' he repeated. 'Preferably Monday morning.'

'No!' she said. 'That plan's really not going to work for me.'

'Then outline a course of action that will,' he countered. 'I need my office back, Professor. I've work to do.'

'Will you be in Sydney on Sunday?' she asked.

'I hope to be.' Plane ticket willing.

'I'll go and get your box from work tomorrow, Dr Tyler. You can pick it up from my private address on Sunday or I will drop it in to wherever you're staying. Does that suit?'

Decisive woman. And yes, it suited him just fine. She gave him her address. They arranged a collection time.

And when he got off the phone, the memory of her voice stayed with him and refused to go away.

'Keep it simple,' Charlotte said to herself for the umpteenth time that morning. Sunday morning, to be exact. Sunday morning at Aurora's, no less, for that was the pickup address she'd given Grey Tyler.

Dr Greyson Tyler was a water weed control specialist. She'd discerned this from the research papers he'd authored and co-authored. Lots of them, and he didn't bother submitting to the smaller journals either. Quality work, all the way.

Maybe she'd read one of his papers years ago and filed his name and that larger than life persona of his somewhere in the dim recesses of her mind. Maybe that was why, when she'd needed an absent fictional fiancé, she'd picked the name Tyler, only she'd used Gil for a first name instead of Greyson. Greyson being far too formidable a name for any fiancé, fictional or otherwise.

Not that it mattered, for within an hour his box would be gone and so would he, and after that there would be no more fictional fiancés *ever* and certainly no doing away with them. 'This I pledge,' she said fervently.

By the time the doorbell finally rang, a good two hours later than expected, Aurora's house was spotless and Charlotte had taken to fretting that Dr Greyson Tyler wouldn't come for his box at all today but would turn up at her workplace tomorrow, thus exposing the entire fictional fiancé debacle to all and sundry, thus sealing her reputation as a complete and utter nutter, and ruining her professional reputation along with it.

She opened the door hastily and found herself staring straight at a broad and muscled chest. She dragged her gaze upwards and finally came to his face. A tough, weathered face, not young and not yet old. Strong black brows framed eyes the colour of bitter coffee, easy on the milk. His hair colour hovered somewhere between that of eyebrows and eyes. He had excellent facial bone structure and an exceptionally fine mouth. A mouth well worth staring at. She had a feeling she'd stared at it before, but where?

Eventually the edge of it tilted up a little and she remembered her manners and stepped back politely and fixed a smile to her own face.

'I'm looking for Professor Greenstone,' he said, his voice a perfect match for the rest of him. Rough around the edges but with a fine baritone centre. Gil had also been in possession of such a voice. A voice to make a woman swoon.

'That would be me,' she said. 'Dr Tyler, I presume?'

'Yes.' His eyes had narrowed. His mouth twisted wryly. 'You're young for an associate professor.'

'My parents were archaeologists,' she said. 'I was raised by my godmother, who was also an archaeologist. I grew up chasing lost cities and ate breakfast, lunch and dinner at tables covered in maps. I was working dig sites by the time I turned six. I had a head start.'

'Sounds like quite a childhood.'

'Worked for me,' she murmured, although it hadn't exactly provided her with an altogether firm grip on reality. Not when there were so many ancient and different realities to choose from. Where *had* she seen his face before? A glossy magazine ad for something sumptuously male and decadently expensive? A magazine article? 'World's Sexiest Scientists', perhaps? Oh, hell. *New Scientist*.

Charlotte sped back in time to a hospital waiting room, and an old waiting room copy of *New Scientist* magazine with an article on water weeds in it. There'd been a picture of the weeds. A picture of this man. She'd skimmed the article while waiting for the specialist to finish with Aurora.

Gil Tyler—fictional fiancé extraordinaire—hadn't been a figment of her imagination at all.

The parts of Gil that hadn't been based on movie superheroes and a long dead father had been based on *this* man.

'Your box is here in the hall,' she said, stepping back and opening wide the huge slab of petrified oak that doubled as a door. 'I taped it back up for your convenience but you're welcome to go through it while you're here if you want to. It's all there.'

The good doctor stepped into the hall and eyed the box balefully.

'Okay, let me rephrase,' she murmured. 'Everything they sent me is in that box, and I'm really sorry if it's not all there.' Charlotte's dismay hit a new low at the thought of Greyson Tyler losing important possessions on her account. 'Extremely sorry.'

Greyson Tyler studied her intently. Finally he put his hand to the back pocket of his trousers, stretching fabric tight across places no well-brought-up woman should be looking. Charlotte averted her gaze and watched the unfolding of the paper instead. He held it out to her. 'I understand you have a fiancé working in PNG and that he and I share a surname.'

Charlotte took the paper from those long strong fingers and reluctantly scanned the email printed on it. The request was a simple one for a photo of the late TJ (Gil) Tyler, botanist, if there was one about. Just as Millie had explained it to her.

'Thing is, PNG is a small place,' he continued conversationally. 'Especially for scientists. I know my colleagues. Your fiancé wasn't one of them. I checked the records. No sign of him there either.'

'It's complicated,' she said, queen of the understatement. 'This email, for instance. Unfortunately, one of my work colleagues sent it on my behalf, without my knowledge, but with the very best intentions.' Charlotte felt herself shrinking beneath that penetrating dark gaze. 'To be fair, the information I gave her about my fiancé wasn't quite correct.'

'Exactly how wrong was it?' he asked silkily.

'You mean on a scale of one to ten with one being almost correct and ten being a whopping great lie with a momentum all its own?'

'If you like.' He could be droll, this man, when he wasn't so busy being stern.

'Ten.'

'And the lie?'

Charlotte shoved her hands in her pockets and moved past him, back through the door so she could stand on the top step of the portico and look out over Aurora's immaculately kept grounds. 'My godmother was dying,' she said, her voice surprisingly even. 'She was the closest thing to family I'd ever had and she was worried about leaving me alone in the world. I invented a fiancé. A botanist, working in PNG. His name was Thaddeus Jeremiah Gilbert Tyler.'

'You named your fiancé Thaddeus?'

'It was 3 a.m. I wasn't exactly thinking straight. Yes, I named him Thaddeus.'

'Go on,' he said.

'Aurora lasted another month. Gil became a regular topic of conversation.'

'Gil?' he queried.

'Thaddeus.' Charlotte closed her eyes, shook her head. Felt her lips curve in memory of some of those late night conversations with Aurora. 'You were right about the name. No one called him Thaddeus except his mother when she was annoyed with him. I called him Gil.'

'Go on.'

'There's not much more to tell,' she murmured, coming back to the present with a start and shooting Greyson an apologetic sideways glance. 'Aurora died. Two days later I did away with Gil, only by that time someone had told my work colleagues about him so the lie continued to grow.

Everyone now thinks I'm mourning both Aurora *and* a fiancé. My colleague Millie went in search of a photo of Gil that I could put up somewhere. To help me grieve, or maybe to help me rejoice in the time I'd spent with him. Something like that.'

'And then?'

'Someone in PNG sent me an office.' Charlotte risked another glance in his direction. Greyson Tyler was staring back at her as if reluctantly, unaccountably fascinated. 'And here you are. I'm not usually this…' She stopped, lost for words.

'Batty?' he said. 'Irresponsible?'

'Like I said, your belongings are in the box in the hall-way,' she muttered. 'I'll reimburse you for the cost of your airfare and your time. I'll make a considerable donation to your research fund. There won't be any more confusion. I'll be telling my boss and my colleagues the truth of the matter tomorrow. Your PNG colleagues too, if that's what it takes. And then there'll be no more lies.' No more good reputation or friends either, but the devil would have his due and Charlotte only had herself to blame. 'You're not married, are you?'

'No.'

'Excellent,' she said faintly.

He'd heard madder explanations. Not often, but it could be done. Grey vacillated between wanting to comfort the apologetic Charlotte and wanting to strangle her.

'Excuse me for a moment,' he muttered, and headed back inside towards the box. The tape gave way easily beneath his hands. Probably his temper showing. Clothes came first and he tossed them aside as befitting their importance. Hard copies of various research papers came next—it looked as if they were all there. He pulled out his laptop and his back-up drives. Reference books, all of them. It was all there.

'What's missing?' Associate Professor Charlotte had joined him, she of the velvet voice and excessive imagination. The horror of losing work was something she appeared to understand.

'Nothing,' he muttered. 'I've decided not to strangle you.'

'You're a rare and generous man,' she said.

'I know.'

'Humility too.'

Sexy velvet voices could be dry as dust and *still* make his blood stir. Who knew? 'Let's not get carried away.' A warning, and not just for her. He started piling books and references back in the box. The good Charlotte retrieved his clothes and handed them to him at the end.

'I've packing tape in the library,' she said, and Grey glanced down the hallway towards the innards of the house. The library. Of course. It was the kind of house that ran to libraries, a billiards room, conservatory, tennis court, pool and gym. Family estate, he figured. Unless she'd made her fortune *before* embarking on a career in archaeology. Possibly as a novelist. *Thaddeus*. Grey snorted. Possibly not.

'Don't worry about the tape. You'd do better worrying about how your work colleagues are going to react when you tell them there's no fiancé, dead or otherwise. You *do* realise that your personal and probably your professional integrity is going to be called into question? Assuming you had some in the first place?'

Charlotte's eyes flashed. Temper temper, and it looked very fine on her but she held her tongue. Not a big woman, by any means, but fragile wasn't a word he would have used to describe her either. Slender, she was that, but she had some generous curves and an abundance of wavy black hair currently tied back in a messy ponytail. She also possessed a heart-shaped face and a creamy complexion that would put Snow White to shame. A wanton's mouth. One that turned a man's mind towards feasting on it. Big doe eyes, with dark curling lashes. 'Are you *really* an archaeologist?'

'Yes,' she said grimly. 'And before you start making comparisons between me and a certain tomb-raiding gun-toting female gaming character, I've heard them all before.'

And been neither flattered nor amused, he deduced. He hefted the box. She held the door open for him.

'Do you need any travel directions to wherever it is you're heading?' she asked. 'Provisions, so you can be on your way? Can of drink? Box of crackers?'

'How did he die?' asked Grey. 'This *fiancé*.'

'Heroically. Very honourably.' No need for details, decided Charlotte. Details were bad. 'It was the least I could do.'

'Has anyone ever told you that your grip on reality's a little shaky?' he murmured.

'Hello,' she said dryly. 'Archaeologist. It's part of the job description.'

A smile from him then. One that chased the sternness right out of him and left devilry in its place. Charlotte stared, drinking in the details. Greyson Tyler was a dangerously handsome man when he wanted to be. Handsomer than Gil.

'Hnh,' she said.

Greyson's smile widened. 'You'll let me know if anything else of mine happens your way?' he said.

'Of course.'

His gaze had shifted to her lips and his smile was fading.

Something else started moving into place. Something fierce and heated.

'Will you be staying in Sydney long?' she all but stuttered. 'Is there a contact number or address I can reach you at?'

'I'll be here for a while,' he said. 'And yes, there is.' Not that he seemed inclined to part with that information. 'This predicament you've got yourself in…'

'Which one?'

'The fake dead fiancé. The lie that just keeps getting bigger.'

'Oh. Right. That predicament.'

'There *is* a way around it without necessarily having to come clean about the lie,' he offered. 'You'd be indebted to me, of course, but I figure that's a small price to pay, and I do happen to know of a way in which you could repay me. All strictly above board and harmless, more or less.'

'What are you suggesting?'

'Resurrection.'

'Pardon?'

'You're not the only one with an ex-fiancé,' he murmured. 'Although mine happens to be real and she's not yet dead. She's also been welcome at my parents' place since childhood. She's part of the family, the daughter my mother never had.'

'No wonder you went paddling up the Sepik afterwards,' said Charlotte. 'Who ended the engagement?'

'I did.'

'Were you heartbroken?'

'Do I look heartbroken?'

'I really don't know you well enough to tell. Was *she* heartbroken?'

'The engagement was a mistake,' said Greyson Tyler curtly. 'Sarah wants a conventional husband. One who's home more often than not. One who's ready to settle down and start a family.'

'How unusual,' murmured Charlotte and wore Greyson's steel-eyed glare with equanimity.

'That's not me. I don't know if it'll ever be me, only Sarah—' He gave a tiny shake of his head. 'Sarah wants to pick up where we left off. With my family's blessing.'

'You're a big boy. Just say no.'

'I have. No one seems to believe me. No one *wants* to believe me. I'm running out of gentle *ways* of saying no, but maybe you can help me. Maybe I can help you.'

'How?'

'I need a woman at my side for a family barbecue next weekend. Preferably one who's ecstatic about me, my way of life, and what I can give her—which is, needless to say, not a lot. A free spirit who can make Sarah and my family believe that everyone should just move on. In return, I'll play your back-from-the-dead fiancé whom you can produce, bicker with, and shortly thereafter cut loose in good conscience. No need to admit your original lie at all. Do we have an agreement?'

Charlotte hesitated, a twinge of something that felt a whole lot like wariness riding her hard. An ex-fiancée who wanted Greyson still, maybe even loved him still. A barbecue at which he—they—would dash her hopes as gently as they could. Except that there would be nothing *gentle* about his ex-fiancée coming face to face with proof positive that Greyson was indeed serious about Sarah needing to move on. 'Are you sure you wouldn't rather have another shot at discussing this between yourselves?' she said. 'Somewhere nice and private? Bring out the steely resolve. Maybe you could say no louder this time.'

'I have,' he said darkly. 'It's not working. Bringing you along might.'

And still Charlotte hesitated.

'Never mind.' His face was closed, his voice clipped. 'Bad idea.'

'Wait,' she said tentatively. 'How long is it since you broke up?'

'Two years.'

'And you really think there's no other way to dissuade her?'

'Look, I don't want to hurt Sarah. I don't want her to feel that she's no longer welcome at my parents' place. I just want her to *see*…'

See being the operative word.

'Couldn't you just *tell* her that you've found someone else?'

Silence from Greyson Tyler. Silence and a bleak black glare. 'You already have,' said Charlotte slowly. 'And now you have to produce her.'

Bingo.

'You're as reality challenged as I am,' she said next.

'Hardly.'

'Oh, give it time.'

Another glare from the behemoth. The one who was offering to help with *her* fiancé problem if she would only help him with his. 'I don't do animosity,' she said firmly. 'If we do this, we do it with as little *hurt* as possible.'

'Agreed.'

'You arrive at my office tomorrow and things seem a little strained between us,' she continued. 'I can take it from there. I attend your family barbecue next weekend, thus providing Sarah with visible evidence that you've moved on, and you can take it from there.'

'Agreed,' he said. 'So do we have a deal?'

More lies aside, Greyson Tyler's suggestion really did seem to solve a multitude of problems. 'We do.'

CHAPTER THREE

THERE was something about waiting for the eminent Dr Greyson Tyler to arrive at her workplace that set Charlotte's jaw to clenching. Correction: the waiting part wasn't the problem. He set her on edge regardless.

She'd been expecting a scientist—a no-nonsense man of formidable intellect and optional physical prowess. Instead she'd encountered Action Man in the flesh, a man so physically fine, quick thinking, and composed in the face of complications that a woman couldn't *help* but wonder what life would be like with a man like that in it. Not steady and predictable, she wagered. Anything but.

Not boring or empty either.

Greyson Tyler was a living, breathing reminder of a life she'd left behind in her quest for inner contentment, security, and peace of mind. Hardly his fault that for all her efforts to settle down, the jury was still out on whether staying in Sydney was making her happy. Where the hell *was* he?

Charlotte had plenty of work to be going on with. Satellite images to look at for a dig site that showed promise. Third-year essays to correct, a lecture to prepare, and no patience this morning for any of it. Greyson was twenty minutes late already. He'd been late yesterday too. The man had a punctuality problem.

That or he'd decided that he didn't need a fake fiancée after all.

Rapping on her open door signalled a visitor and Charlotte turned to see who it was.

Millie.

'Morning tea time,' said Millie.

Indeed it was, and the perfect time for introducing a formerly dead pretend fiancé to her colleagues, but Greyson Tyler did not put in an appearance during the break.

Gil would have *never* been so tawdry.

But when she and Millie walked back along the corridor after the break, Charlotte discovered she had a visitor. A visitor who felt at home enough to plant his rear in her chair and his boots on her filing cabinet while he browsed through one of her archaeology journals.

Millie stopped. Stared.

Greyson Tyler glanced up, nodded to Millie, and favoured Charlotte with a deliciously slow smile; an invitation to come play with him if she dared.

'You made it,' she said icily.

'Of course.' Greyson's smile widened. Lucifer would have been proud. 'I always do. Eventually.'

Millie was still staring. Charlotte figured introductions were in order. 'Millie, this is Tyler. He arrived home yesterday, rather unexpectedly. Tyler, meet Millie. Historian, map muse, and friend.'

'But…' Millie slid Charlotte a lightning glance before returning her attention to the figure in the chair. 'You're not dead.'

'No,' said Grey. 'Well spotted.'

'Apparently there was some confusion on that score,' murmured Charlotte.

'But…that's *wonderful*!' said Millie on firmer footing.

'I'm glad *someone* thinks so,' said Grey.

Greyson Tyler played the part of antagonist exceptionally well, decided Charlotte. The man was a natural.

With fluid grace, Greyson found his feet and held out his hand towards Millie, his smile a study in warmth and friendliness. 'Charlotte's had a rough few months, what with one thing and another,' he offered in that chocolate coated baritone. 'Thanks for helping her out.'

Millie shook his hand as if awestruck. Millie blushed, caught Charlotte's eye and blushed some more.

'How long are you planning on staying angry with him?' Millie asked her.

'A while,' said Charlotte.

'Good luck with that.' Millie slid another helpless smile in Greyson's direction. 'I'm so glad you weren't eaten by marauding tribesmen,' she told him. 'Did you manage to prevent the village daughters from being kidnapped as well?'

Grey blinked. A muscle ticced beside his mouth. 'Yes,' he said finally.

'Hard to stay angry with a hero,' said Millie.

'Oh, it's not that hard,' said Charlotte.

Stifling a grin, Millie left.

Charlotte shut the door in Millie's wake, took a steadying breath, and turned to face the man currently dominating her office space. His charming friendly smile had disappeared. The formidable Greyson Tyler had returned and he seemed out of sorts.

'I think that went well, don't you?' she said lightly.

'You told them I'd been *eaten*? By *cannibals*?'

'Not *you*,' she said soothingly. 'Gil. And of course nothing was ever *certain*.'

'And they *believed* you?'

'It happens,' said Charlotte.

'Sixty years ago. Maybe.'

'What's a few decades? Besides, it's a moot point. You're back, alive and kicking and about to become my ex-fiancé. You need to embrace the bigger picture here.'

'I'll refrain from mentioning what I think you need,' he said.

'Greyson, all is well. Your work here is done and I do sincerely thank you for it,' she said earnestly. 'I'm still prepared to attend this barbecue with you but if you'd rather not… If you've decided you no longer need a fictional fiancée, or that I'm too irresponsible and that no one's going to believe we're an item anyway, it doesn't have to happen. Your call.'

Greyson's gaze grew intent. Whatever other flaws he had, there was no denying that the man could focus intently on something when he wanted to. 'You welshing on me, Greenstone? I come through for you and you don't reciprocate? Is that how you repay your debts?'

'I didn't say that,' she said evenly, never mind the erratic beating of her heart. 'I'm simply giving you the opportunity to reconsider your options. Fictional fiancés are more trouble than they're worth—trust me on this. I'm doing you a favour by pointing this out.'

'You're very kind,' he said smoothly. 'I propose an experiment. Something that lets me decide if bringing you along to meet the family is going to work.' He drew closer. Close enough for her to feel the heat in that big lean body of his. Close enough for her to catch the scent of him. Tantalisingly male, undeniably appealing. And then there was his mouth. Such a tempting mouth.

'Kiss me,' he murmured, and her eyes flew to his.

'Excuse me?'

'That's the experiment,' he said. 'If there's no chemistry we're square. Finished.' His lips moved closer. 'Through.' Greyson's lips brushed hers, and Charlotte drew a ragged breath. 'No barbecue.' And then his lips were on hers, warm and coaxing, not demanding, not yet.

Teasing, those lips of his.

Practised, the hand that came up to cradle her skull and position her for deeper invasion, only he didn't invade, not yet.

Torture first.

Slow, savouring torture as his tongue traced her lips, only to withdraw once she'd parted them for him. His lips playing at the edge of her upper lip now while she gasped for breath and clutched at his forearms for balance, only to have his skin beneath her palms play havoc with those senses too.

His eyes stayed open, observing, always observing, coolly watching her come apart beneath his ministrations.

And then he closed his eyes, slid his mouth over hers and simply took.

He wasn't supposed to devour her, thought Grey with what little coherent thought he had left. He'd only meant to test her, not match her uninhibited response and raise the stakes by tabling a whole lot of mindless hunger as well. Too long without a woman, that had to be it, as he buried his hands in her silken tresses, his lips not leaving hers as he took what he needed and what he would have by way of supplication and desire.

She didn't protest. The ragged husky sounds she made weren't sounds of protest. The way she gave her mouth over to him, as if savouring every last drop of his invasion, wasn't objection. She wrapped her arms around his neck as he lifted her up, both hands on her buttocks urging her legs around his waist and she obliged him and kept right on kissing him. Another gasp escaped her, one he echoed as hardness found a home. Too many clothes. Way too much urgency. He wasn't a small man, not by any means. He usually had more care for a woman's comfort. He usually made sure to harness his strength and turn it to tenderness.

There was no tenderness here, just sensuality unleashed and Grey wanted more, and more again, and Charlotte gave willingly. Locking her legs around his waist she rode his hard length through two sets of clothing and slayed him with her abandon.

It was Charlotte who guided them back to reality.

'Enough,' she muttered, and when he bared his teeth against her cheek on a groan of pure frustration, 'Greyson, stop.' Grey's body protested but he gentled his hold on her and held still while she nestled her forehead into the curve of his shoulder, her body trembling as she sought to master her desire and his. 'I'm not saying no.' Her lips and breath were warm against the skin of his neck, that sex-soaked voice doing nothing to aid her cause. 'I'm saying not here, and not now. Let's not be insane.'

Rich, coming from her.

But he slid her down gently, let her find her feet and step away and put some distance between them. One foot and then another until reason and caution returned.

'What just happened?' she asked warily.

'You want the standard biology lecture or shall we just summarise and say that the dopamine and adrenaline kicked in? Hard.'

'In other words, just an ordinary everyday biological response to sexual stimulus,' she murmured and leaned against her workbench. 'Nothing more.'

'Exactly.' Thank God for analytical minds. 'I may be a little overdue for release in that particular arena. I've been out of touch with female company for a while. Nothing for you to worry about. Nothing I can't control.'

She sent him a look, dark amusement running deep.

'So I'll pick you up Sunday morning at around eleven thirty,' he said, ignoring his growing unease when it came to spending any amount of time with the delectably loopy Charlotte Greenstone. 'It'll take us an hour to get there. Barbecue starts at one. I figure we can be gone by three.'

'You're sure about this?' She folded her arms across her slim waist.

'I'm sure.' More or less.

'How would you like me dressed?'

Greyson blinked. 'Do you normally ask a man this question?'

'Normally, I can figure it out on my own. With you, all bets are off.'

He still didn't have an answer to her question.

'I'm not asking you for your colour preferences, Greyson. I'm asking you for your social status. I realise it doesn't show, but I'm not without wealth. The kind that takes generations to acquire. You want me to wear it or not?'

'Up to you,' he said with a shrug. 'My family is solidly middle class. My mother's a paediatrician and my father's a mechanical engineer currently contracted to the Australian Defence Force. My ex is a psychiatrist. We're heading for a holiday house on the banks of the Hawkesbury. It's private, sprawling, and comfortable in a totally different way from the showpiece you inhabit. There'll be good wine, home-cooked food, and enough conversation to fill any gaps. Is that enough information?'

'Plenty,' she murmured, her gaze turning speculative. 'Believe it or not, I just want to get this right and hopefully get the job you want me to do done with as little bloodshed as possible. Do you have any siblings?'

'No.'

'Anything else I should know in advance? Your ex-fiancée, Sarah. Will she be protective of you?'

'Not without analysing the situation and every possible response to it first.'

'Marvellous,' muttered Charlotte, with the lift of a sweetly pointed chin. 'You do realise that a psychiatrist will probably have a field day with me. I'm not without my eccentricities.'

'Really? Who'd have guessed?' Time to leave before he closed the distance between them and set his lips to the slender curve of her neck. 'Look at it this way, it'll give her something to do. Oh, and before I forget your what-to-wear question,' he said as he opened her office door, 'my favourite colour's green.'

CHAPTER FOUR

GREEN it was, and a vibrant tree-frog green at that, shot through with yellows and vivid reds, pinks, and purples. Okay, so maybe calling her silk spaghetti-strapped sundress green was a stretch. Maybe green was only *one* of the colours splashed on it, but it was suitably bohemian, flattering to the figure, and inviting to the touch.

The matching manilas or Portuguese slave bracelets Charlotte wore at her wrists were a particularly nice touch, considering her services for the day had been bought and paid for. Part of Aurora's eclectic collection of antiquities, the beaten brass bracelets could almost be classified as green and would hopefully give Sarah the psychiatrist something to dwell on.

Just one more reason to make Sarah reconsider whether she wanted to renew a relationship with a man whose current paramour indulged his every whim.

Tedious business, the indulging of a man's whims.

Charlotte's make-up was subtle and she'd decided against perfume. Her demeanour was obliging; she'd been practising all morning.

Time to get this over with. This task she had no taste for.

This dashing of another woman's hopes and dreams.

* * *

As far as anthropological experiments were concerned, Grey had a strong suspicion that this one was ripe for failure. Too many variables. Far too many unknowns. Social interaction between him and Charlotte had been volatile, at best. Add the pretence of a relationship, his parents, and an ex-fiancée to the mix, and the impending family barbecue had all the hallmarks of social disaster.

When he drove up Charlotte's gravelled circular driveway and she looked up from her watering of the plants beneath the portico and smiled, he groaned aloud.

He'd ordered a free-spirited woman. By Charlotte's translation, this seemed to mean a golden-limbed goddess wrapped in a slip of a dress that dazzled the eyes. A wild profusion of wavy black hair tumbled to her waist and showcased her dress to perfection. Completing the outfit were flat sandals that looked suspiciously like ballet slippers, and huge grey-tinted sunglasses courtesy of someone's Elton John collection.

Bring on the circus.

He brought the car to a standstill. A hired, late-model four door Toyota, nothing special, hopefully reliable. Charlotte cut the tap, rolled up the hose on its reel and tucked hose and reel into a low cupboard, seemingly built for that purpose. Money, and lots of it, thought Grey. Enough to make conforming to society's rules optional, never mind the tidy hose arrangement. It might be worth discussing a few rules of engagement before they reached his parents' place. Spell out just what he expected of an unconventional yet perfectly acceptable partner in deception.

Charlotte collected up a handbag and wrap from beside the front door. She made sure the door was locked and made her way towards the Toyota. She bent down and smiled at him through the window, showing even white teeth and an abundance of free-spirited cleavage.

She made no move to get in the car.

Gritting his own teeth, Grey slid from the car, strode around it and hauled the door open for her. 'Why couldn't you have been a feminist?' he said.

'Why on earth would I want to be a feminist?' she muttered as she slid into the seat and waited for him to close the door. 'Where's the power in that?'

He shut the door. Gently. He got back in the car.

'You'll notice I'm not currently wearing a bra,' she said briskly.

Oh, he'd noticed.

'That's because the bodice of this dress fulfils that function, not because it's a feminist convention of the late last century.'

'Noted,' he said.

'I would, however, have made a wonderful suffragette,' she told him. 'There are *many* principles of equality that I adhere to.'

'Wonderful,' he said dryly. 'Power-based selective feminism. Can't wait to experience that.'

'Oh, I dare say you already have,' she murmured. 'How long were you engaged?'

'One year. And Sarah opens her own doors.'

'As is her choice,' said Charlotte magnanimously. 'Did you live with her?'

'No. I spent most of that time in PNG. In my defence, Sarah knew I'd committed to a three year project there *before* we became engaged.'

'Perhaps she thought she could tolerate the wait,' said Charlotte. 'And discovered otherwise.'

'Yes,' he said heavily, and won several points for honesty. 'That's pretty much what happened.'

Not a comfortable topic of conversation for Greyson Tyler, decided Charlotte. Plenty of skeletons in that cupboard.

'Sarah's a smart woman,' he continued. 'Capable. Loyal. Lovely. I want her to be happy. I want her to realise that calling off our engagement was a good decision and that one day she'll meet someone who *can* fulfil all her needs, not just some of them.'

'Idealistic,' murmured Charlotte.

'Practical,' he countered.

'If you say so. You know what's interesting when you speak of your Sarah?' said Charlotte. 'You never speak of passion. Or longing. Or needing to wake up beside her. Did you never feel that? Not even in the beginning?'

Grey stayed stubbornly silent.

'I see,' she said gently. 'Then I guess she *is* better off without you.'

They drove the next twenty kilometres in silence.

'So when did we meet?' asked Charlotte, determinedly breaking the silence.

'Three months ago when I was in Brisbane for a conference. I stayed a fortnight longer than planned because of you. We kept in touch. How does that sound?'

'Plausible. I'm liking the implied passion. Let's face it; you're not offering commitment, progeny, or fiscal support. There's got to be *something* in it for me.'

'There is. A back-from-the-dead fiancé who suffered the ignominy of almost being eaten by cannibals.'

'Something else,' she said, not above a little needling of her own. 'I'm thinking that if I really was the free-spirited type, I'd probably only want you for the sex. Outrageously intimate sex of the most delectable kind. The kind of passionate tour de force a woman would go out of her way to encounter.' Charlotte lifted her sunglasses and favoured him with a sultry glance. 'How does that sound?'

'I've no complaints,' he said gruffly.

'Excellent,' she murmured. 'I *do* hope you can keep your end of the pretence up.'

'It's up.' God, what was it about this woman's voice that had him reacting like an oversexed schoolboy? Grey suffered that knowing gaze of hers drifting down his body in silence. He suffered the lift of her elegant eyebrow and the tiny tilt of generously curved lips.

'Stop it,' he muttered.

'Practice makes perfect,' she said airily. 'I'm a method actor.'

He put the radio on, a man in need of a diversion. 'Tell me about your work,' he said, and then just as quickly decided against hearing it. Given the effect of her voice on his body, it was probably best if she didn't speak at all. 'No. I've changed my mind. Don't speak. Take a nap or something. Pretend you had a tiring night.'

'I *did* have a tiring night,' she said. 'I dreamed of you.'

Greyson Tyler quite unknowingly brought out the worst in her, decided Charlotte as they drove up a steep and winding track to his parents' weekender on the river. Tall gums and rocky undergrowth stretched before them and a vast river flowed behind them, placid and serene. None of it could stop the butterflies from starting up in her stomach. None of it could match the man beside her when it came to arresting views. He'd dressed casually in old jeans and a white linen shirt with a round neck. The shirt *could* have looked effeminate, but not on those shoulders, and not with that face.

No, with those shoulders and that face and that lean

and tight rear end of his, the metro shirt served only to emphasise the blatant masculinity of the body beneath.

'Ready?' he asked gruffly.

'Ready,' she said with far more confidence than the situation warranted. 'Just as soon as you open the car door.'

He got out and came round to her side of the car and opened the door. He put his hand out to assist her graceful exit. He even managed to hide his impatience with the whole antiquated process.

Almost.

'Thank you, Greyson,' she said magnanimously as she flowed out of the car and into his arms, one hand still in his and one hand covering his heart as she pressed her lips to that strong square jaw. 'You'll figure out this game yet.'

'I already have,' he murmured. 'It's about torture, and touch, and it's dangerous.' His mouth hovered over hers. His eyes promised retribution. 'Don't say I didn't warn you.'

'And a gentleman is born.' Charlotte smiled in slow challenge, but peripheral movement made her glance beyond Greyson. A trim, well-preserved older woman had come out onto the deck of the house and stood watching. 'I think your mother's watching us.'

'Good,' he murmured, and kissed her. Not swiftly or perfunctorily, but with a sensual abandon that a mother probably didn't need to see.

'How am I doing so far on the led-astray-by-passion front?' he murmured when he'd finished with her.

'Quite well,' she offered, her words little more than a strangled squeak. 'Mind you, Gilbert would never have subjected me to such kisses in front of his mother. Gil had more sense.'

'Pity he wasn't *real*,' said Greyson silkily.

Cheap shot. So was the hand she deliberately let brush across the well-packed front of his jeans as she sailed past him and summoned up what she hoped was a meet-the-parents smile. Charlotte wasn't all that familiar with parents, hers or anyone else's, but mentioning this tiny snippet to Greyson *now* would only alarm him.

'You must be Charlotte,' said the older woman with a smile. Not entirely friendly, not exactly brimming with antagonism either. Greyson's mother was reserving judgement. 'We've heard a lot about you of late.'

'She's lying,' said Greyson, coming up the deck stairs behind Charlotte and putting his hand to the small of her back as he leaned in and pressed a light kiss to his mother's perfectly powdered cheek. 'I told her you lectured at the university and that she'd be meeting you on Sunday. That's *all* I told her.'

'Thus ensuring a week's worth of rampant speculation,' Greyson's mother said dryly before turning her attention back to Charlotte. 'Call me Olivia,' she said. 'And I promise to limit my curiosity to the basics. Age. Weight. Intentions...'

Charlotte twirled on the ball of her ballet slippers and ran smack bang into Greyson's chest.

'The door's that way,' he rumbled.

'I know.' She stared up at him, more than a little panicked. 'I really don't think I can do this.'

'Coward,' he said next. 'Think of your reputation.'

'I'm thinking it's shattered beyond repair anyway,' she said to his shirt covered chest.

'Then think of mine.'

'Yours seems pretty robust from where I'm standing.'

'Not if you run out on me.' Greyson put his lips to her ear. 'Please, Charlotte. Just follow my lead.'

Charlotte didn't stand a chance against a pleading Greyson Tyler. Charlotte straightened. Charlotte turned. Greyson's mother stood waiting by the sliding door into the house. Maybe intimidation came naturally to her. Or maybe Charlotte was just oversensitive when it came to mothers and wanting to impress them and knowing instinctively that she wasn't going to. 'I'm sorry,' she said, summoning a smile. 'Slight moment of panic on my part. I hadn't really thought through my intentions towards your son. Nothing to worry about though. I'm pretty sure I only want him for the sex.' Nothing but the truth.

Olivia blinked, and turned her gaze on her son.

'What?' he said blandly and ushered Charlotte through the door. 'It's a start.'

There were more people inside. Neighbours and family friends, Greyson's father. Half a dozen faces in all. Someone handed Charlotte a frosty glass of white wine, and Greyson a beer.

'Thank you,' murmured Charlotte, and promptly drained half of hers. Greyson was far more restrained. He only took one mouthful of his.

'I hope you're not lactose intolerant or allergic to seafood,' said Olivia, offering up what looked to be trout dip with rosemary flatbread on the side. 'Grey didn't seem to know.'

'I eat almost anything.' Charlotte tried a mouthful of bread and dip. Nodded as she chewed and swallowed, with every eye still firmly fixed upon her. Perhaps they were assessing her manners. Perhaps they'd overheard the sex comment. 'This is delicious. Thank you.'

Grey's mother smiled warily and moved on, offering the plate around to all her guests. Conversation resumed. Gazes drifted away. Charlotte took a deep breath. Follow his lead, Greyson had told her, only Greyson was now being talked at by a grey-haired gent who seemed wholly disinclined to include her in the conversation. Charlotte sipped at her drink more cautiously now and surveyed her surroundings. Large covered deck, an array of comfortable chairs. Stainless-steel gas barbecue groaning with sizzling seafood kebabs. Lots of older couples and one other younger woman around Charlotte and Greyson's age, standing a short distance away. A beautiful buttoned-down blonde with forest-green eyes and an air of quiet suffering.

Probably Sarah.

Bohemian, Greyson had requested of Charlotte. Free-spirited. Now she knew why. The contrast between herself and the lovely Sarah couldn't have been more extreme.

Sarah smiled tentatively at her. Charlotte smiled back.

Awkward.

'Hi, I'm Sarah,' said Sarah, in the absence of anyone else willing to make the introduction. 'The ex-fiancée.'

'Charlotte,' said Charlotte. 'Greyson's...friend.'

'I know,' said Sarah quietly, and that was that. Or maybe not, because Sarah was still speaking. 'How long have you known him?'

'A few months.'

'Not long.'

'No, not long.' Not when compared to a lifetime.

'Long enough to fall in love with him?' Sarah asked next.

'Sarah...' said Charlotte, helpless to reply in the face of the other woman's pain. Where the hell was Greyson? When did it become *her* job to break this woman's heart?

'It's okay,' said Sarah. 'Heaven knows he's easy enough to love.'

'Oh, not at the moment,' murmured Charlotte. 'At the moment I'm more of a mind to wring his neck. You?'

Sarah looked startled. Then a tiny smile appeared. The shrug of an elegant shoulder. 'Now that you mention it...'

'Exactly.' Charlotte smiled in full. 'The man's a menace.'

The man in question looked up from his discussion with the white-haired patriarch. The man in question paled a little when he saw them together. Kudos to him when he rapidly excused himself and headed their way.

About damn time.

'He minds you,' said Sarah. 'He's nervous.'

'How can you tell?' asked Charlotte.

'Shoulders,' said Sarah. 'His carriage. The way he keeps glancing at you. He can't read you. He doesn't know what you want.' Greyson's ex glanced back at Charlotte. 'That's interesting.'

'No, I'm pretty sure that's just me,' said Charlotte. 'Hard for Greyson to know what I want when I hardly know myself. I really can't blame him for that one.'

'Blame who?' said Greyson, reaching them.

'You,' said Charlotte and smothered a smile when his eyes narrowed upon her. 'It's okay though. I've decided not to. For now.'

'Good of you,' he murmured.

Sarah was watching them closely. Sarah the psychiatrist who'd known how to read Greyson since childhood and who in the space of a three-minute conversation had already unearthed Charlotte's greatest flaw. 'Sarah and I have been getting acquainted.' Charlotte bestowed on him a very level look.

Greyson bestowed on the lovely Sarah a very level look. Sarah blushed and looked away.

'I might go and see if Olivia needs any help with serving the food,' said Sarah finally, after a long and awkward pause. 'Nice meeting you, Charlotte. Grey.' And then Sarah was gone.

'Nice manners,' murmured Charlotte.

'What did she want?'

'I guess she wanted to meet me. Get it over and done with.'

'Don't underestimate her, Charlotte.' For a moment Greyson looked troubled. Concerned, and not for Sarah. 'For all Sarah's good points, she's not without claws.'

'Greyson. Sweet man.' Did he really think he was telling her something she didn't know? Charlotte smiled, really smiled at him and had the pleasure of seeing Greyson relax and smile back. 'No woman is.'

'So...' he murmured. 'You know what you're doing, then.'

'Hardly,' she murmured. 'Do you?'

'Sometimes. Right now, for example, I'm about to introduce you to my father. He's the one over there captaining the barbecue.'

But Charlotte hung back. 'Is he a Sarah fan too?'

'He's very fond of her, yes.'

Great.

'Relax. He'll be fine,' said Greyson as if reading her mind. 'And so will you.'

For an Associate Professor of Archaeology, with all the staidness the position implied, Charlotte Greenstone didn't hold back when it came to playing the part of free-spirited bohemian. She could tell a story of old bones and bring to life the heat and the dust and the excitement along with it. She could open a person up and rifle around inside until she found something they could both discuss with passion and verve. She had manners, and a great deal of charm, some of which was polished, and some of it innate.

Grey watched Charlotte bespell his father within minutes of her starting up a conversation with him about the vagaries of catapults versus castle walls. He watched her as she talked oysters with his father's fishing buddy and recipes with his wife. He watched his mother's friends tread carefully with her, wanting to find fault with her manners or her demeanour, and discovering to their consternation that they could not.

His mother remained aloof, never mind Charlotte's many attempts to initiate conversation and find common ground.

Chillingly, publicly unimpressed.

The meal came and went and the hours ground by. People began to make noises about leaving. Charlotte asked if there was anything she could do when it came to the clearing of tables or general tidying up. Grey frowned as Sarah immediately stepped in and began clearing and Olivia waved Charlotte away, telling her to sit and relax and continue telling tales.

Telling tales…

As if nothing she'd said so far could be trusted.

Charlotte smiled politely. She didn't so much as flinch as she settled back into playing the role of carefree companion and confident lover, and doing herself a disservice in the process, for there was more to her than that. Far more depth than he'd ever suspected.

Maybe it was time to leave.

Grey eased Charlotte away from the other guests until they reached the deck railing. He pointed out the various landmarks and she leaned her shoulder against his and showed every indication of hanging on his every word. He hadn't touched her since their earlier kiss. He hadn't been game. Now he turned his back on the view and spread his arms along the railing. Not quite an embrace, but an invitation for Charlotte to take what she would from him. Shelter, if she wanted it. Protection if she felt the need. Or anything else she might want to avail herself of.

Charlotte traced her fingers along the inside of his arm, up to his elbow and back, and when she reached his hand she covered it with her own, so soft and slim against the rough squareness of his. He liked the contrast. He liked a lot of things about this woman.

'Ready to go?' he murmured.

Relief crossed her face and was gone in an instant but this time he saw it. Charlotte Greenstone was more than ready to leave the family embrace and probably had been for hours.

'Yes.'

'C'mere,' he murmured and drew her towards him, touching his lips to her hair as she nestled against him as if she'd been there a thousand times and would be there a thousand more before they were through. 'You should have said.'

'It's your show.'

Yes, but it was *her* identity that was taking the battering.

They made their farewells after that. Sarah receiving Grey's guarded goodbye with a tight-lipped smile and eyes that wished him to hell. He hadn't encouraged Sarah's attentions over the course of the afternoon. Sarah hadn't given chase, hadn't made a scene, hadn't singled out Charlotte again. Sarah waited, that was all, and Grey wished to hell she wouldn't.

'Where to next with your work?' asked his father as he and Olivia saw them to the door.

'Could be Borneo,' said Grey. 'Could stay here a while.

Plans are pretty fluid at the moment.' He slid Charlotte a quick glance. Charlotte picked it up and responded with a smile.

'Borneo's lovely,' she enthused, playing the Boheme and playing it well. 'Wonderful place to visit and to work. My godmother and I spent half a year there once, when I was a child. Think of the history.'

'Think of the malaria,' said Olivia dryly. 'What were you and your godmother doing there?'

'Just looking,' said Charlotte. 'We did that a lot. Thank you for having me to lunch.' She didn't say she enjoyed it. Olivia didn't say, 'Do come again.'

Women.

Grey wasn't used to a pensive Charlotte Greenstone. A woman who wore her beauty effortlessly, almost unconsciously, but who'd grown quieter and more reflective with every passing kilometre. As if lunch with his parents and Sarah and all the rest had drained her dry.

'I'm sorry about my mother,' he said, after another fifteen kilometres of silence.

'Mothers are protective of their young,' she said quietly. 'You don't have to be a biology major to get that. Anyway, it's not as if I'll be seeing her again.' Charlotte closed her eyes as if to shut out reality. 'May I offer up a little bit of advice?'

'Go ahead.'

'When you *do* find a woman who interests you, introduce her to your family gradually. Try one limb at a time; or one family member at a time. Don't involve Sarah, not at the start. It does no one any favours.'

'Noted,' he murmured. 'And thank you.' He'd do well to keep his eyes on the road and off his companion. His wildly beautiful companion with hidden depths. 'Are you hungry? We could stop somewhere on the way home. I did promise you dinner.'

'I can't eat any more today,' she said. 'Your mother sets a fine table.'

'You have to eat something later on.'

'I might have a cognac nightcap.'

'That's not food.'

'Want to bet?'

They drove in silence after that, apart from a murmured comment here and there. When they got to the outskirts of Sydney, Charlotte surprised him yet again by requesting that he drop her at an inner city Rocks address rather than the one he'd picked her up from.

She directed him into a steeply descending driveway, dug a set of keys from her handbag, and pressed a remote switch attached to the key ring. The eight-foot wrought-iron driveway gates began to ease open. A heavy-duty garage Roll-A-Door began to open further down the drive. 'Who lives here?'

'Me,' she said as Grey drove down into a spacious underground car park with room for a dozen or so vehicles. 'The house at Double Bay belongs to Aurora. At least, it did. Now it's mine, only I couldn't face going there tonight. She'd have been disappointed in me today, I think. In the hurt I caused, no matter how much better off Sarah's going to be without you. Too many lies. Far too many lies of late, and they just keep getting bigger. You can park there.'

He did as suggested, brooding over her remarks as he strode around the car to open the door for her.

She smiled, briefly, as she got out of the car and he closed the door behind her, but there was no leaning into him as there had been for his parents' benefit. No playing of power games.

'I'm sorry about today,' he said gruffly. 'I shouldn't have dragged you into this.'

'You didn't. We had a deal. A good deal—one I entered into willingly.' She offered up a small smile. 'Don't mind me if I seem a bit morose. It'll pass.'

He hoped so.

'Would you care to come up for a coffee?' she said next. 'I've no agenda, no ulterior motive other than I don't think much of my own company these days and I do my best to avoid it. You could tell me about your research. About what you hope to find in Borneo.'

Grey hesitated.

'Never mind,' she said quietly. 'It's not mandatory. We're square now. And you probably have other places to be.'

Somewhere between this morning and now, Charlotte's confidence had taken a hammering and self-derision had found purchase. His doing, not hers, and he cursed himself for not seeing, not giving any thought whatsoever to Charlotte's feelings about the role he'd asked her to play and the hits she would take on his behalf.

'You should know that a research scientist never misses an opportunity to expound on his work,' he offered gravely. 'You don't even have to be an appreciative audience. You just have to be awake. And, yes, I'll join you for coffee.'

They stepped into a lift and went up a few floors and came out onto a landing with only two doors leading from it, one of which was labelled 'Fire Escape.'

Charlotte's penthouse apartment boasted a million-dollar close-up view of Sydney Harbour Bridge, framed by enormous, double—or triple—glazed tinted windows. White was the predominant colour in the apartment; white walls and ceilings, white marble floors, white kitchen fixtures and benches and a snow-white leather lounge. And then, as if someone had taken exception to the designer palate and vowed to melt it down, an eclectic array of paintings, sculptures, books, tapestries and floor rugs in every imaginable colour and from every imaginable historical period had been added to the mix.

He stopped in front of a painting formed entirely of various coloured oil paints dripped onto a canvas in no particular order.

'Do you like it?' she said.

'What is it?'

'Abstract art. Jackson Pollock's finest. It's whatever you want it to be.'

'Handy,' he murmured. 'You *own* this?'

Charlotte nodded. 'It was my grandmother's. Lots of rumours about how she came to own it. My favourite one is that she and Pollock were friends and that she won it from him in a card game. Rumour has it they were initially playing with coins from the Roman Empire. As the stakes got higher, the currency of the realm went twentieth century.'

'What exactly does a person throw in the pot to match a Jackson Pollock painting?' he asked.

'Could have been the Dali,' she said.

Of course. The Dali. 'Family wealth, you said. Just how much family wealth is there?'

'Plenty,' she said dryly. 'My great grandfather was in shipping. My grandmother added luxury liners to the mix and then divested herself of the lot when she hit her fifties. Said it had sapped the life out of her. She turned philanthropist, gave a lot of her possessions away, but she still left my mother extremely well provided for. She urged my mother to follow her heart. My mother took her advice, chose my father and archaeology, and by all accounts was ecstatically happy with both. My parents died in a light aircraft crash in Peru when I was five.'

'Long time ago,' he murmured.

'So it was. I usually went everywhere with them but that day they decided to leave me at the hotel with Aurora.'

'This is the Aurora who died recently? Your godmother? The one you invented a fiancé for?'

Charlotte nodded. 'Aurora was an archaeologist like my parents. Fortunately for me, they'd also named her as my guardian in their wills. From then on, I went where Aurora went and that was everywhere. You take milk in your coffee?'

'No, thanks,' he said. 'How long have you worked at Sydney Uni?'

'Five years.'

'And this associate professorship, it allows for the kind of travel you're used to?'

'No, it's a desk job.'

'And you're not fed up with that?'

'Not yet.' She set spoons and a bowl of sugar on the counter. A pewter sugar bowl with dragonfly handles. 'I like the stability. I like the people I work closely with. I even like the routine, and I can usually tolerate the politics. And what with communications these days, field teams can get photos and data to me and I can make comment within minutes if required.'

'You wouldn't rather *be* there?'

'I've been there,' she murmured. 'I travelled that road for twenty-three years. When Aurora retired, I lost enthusiasm for it. It just wasn't the same without her and I didn't want to continue on alone. I hate being alone.' Charlotte absent-mindedly brushed dark curls from her face. 'I can play your free-spirited bohemian friend to perfection, Greyson. I have many role models I can look to for inspiration. Heaven knows, my boss would be ecstatic if I went back out into the field for a while. Problem is, I'm very fond of my settled existence. Of being among familiar faces. I think that in the absence of family I look to the community for a sense of belonging. Of place. I need to feel connected to something, whereas you…you need to be free. It's why we'd never gel in real life. It's why, deep down inside, I'm no better suited to you than Sarah is.'

'Thanks for the warning.'

'My pleasure,' she said gravely. 'Doesn't mean I can't enjoy your company. Doesn't mean that when it comes to a short-term liaison I couldn't be tempted to take my fill of you. You *are* a spectacularly beautiful specimen and you have some very fine qualities.'

Charlotte murmured something else but Grey's brain had ceased functioning the moment she'd mentioned the words *short-term liaison* and *tempted*.

He tracked Charlotte's every move as she set the coffee machine to working. Moments later a steaming cup of fragrant coffee-beaned joy sat on the gleaming granite-topped kitchen counter in front of him. Too hot for drinking, so he added sugar and stirred and Charlotte did the same to hers. The porcelain teaspoons had porcelain ladybirds on them.

'So, Borneo next,' she said eventually.

'Maybe. There's write-up work to do on the PNG project first. Reports. Papers. Probably some presentation work.'

'Ah, yes. The Glory,' she murmured. 'A scientist's pleasure.'

There were other types of pleasure.

'About your thoughts on short-term liaisons,' he muttered, and suffered her knowing gaze and her delicately raised eyebrow with dogged determination. 'What are they?'

'Would you like an in-depth analysis or just the summary?' she enquired sweetly.

'Just the summary.'

'Okay. Assuming that both participants are free from all other romantic entanglements, I'm reasonably in favour of flings as a legitimate means of providing temporary companionship and sexual satisfaction.'

'That's a very bohemian outlook for a woman who eschews a carefree life.'

'If you say so. Of course, even a temporary partner has to fit certain criteria. A different set of criteria from that expected of a life partner.'

'Of course,' murmured Grey. 'Do you have a list?'

'Of course.' She didn't elaborate, just smiled. Charlotte Greenstone knew how to make a man work for what he wanted.

'Let me guess,' he murmured as he set his coffee aside and leaned over the counter towards her, his mouth mere inches from her own. 'You need to be attracted to him.'

'Well, naturally.'

'He needs to satisfy you sexually.'

'Goes without saying.' Her gaze had settled on his lips. 'I'm thinking we'd be good to go in that respect.'

'Does he need to be wealthier than you?'

'No, but he does need to feel secure enough in his circumstances for my wealth not to intimidate him. I don't need to dine at the most expensive restaurant in the city. I don't need to be lavished with expensive gifts. What I do expect, when a temporary liaison invites me out to dinner or drinks or a show, is that he pays for it. When I do the inviting, payment will naturally fall to me.'

'Sounds very fair-minded for a woman who insists on having her car door opened for her.'

'I'm a woman of contrasts,' she said. 'Also a big fan of gentlemanly manners. A short-term liaison candidate would require those too, or at least be willing to learn some.'

'Anything else?' he asked silkily.

'Yes. A temporary lover would have limited input when it comes to my long-term plans and how I choose to live my life. There'd be no trying to turn me to his way of thinking. No major compromises required. Asking for such would almost certainly signal the *end* of the liaison.'

'Have you a position on time limits for such an association?' he asked. He'd never met a woman quite so fond of rules and regulations when it came to personal interaction. The scientist in him was intrigued by the need for such protective barriers. The suitor in him regarded it as a challenge.

'How long they're going to be in the area usually dictates the length of the association,' she murmured. 'I don't encourage long distance relationships, temporary or otherwise.'

'Yet you still invented long-distance Gil.'

'Well, I could hardly invent a fiancé who lived in Sydney. I'd have had to produce him. And lest you get the impression that I enter into temporary liaisons lightly and without careful forethought, I don't.'

'I'm getting that,' he said dryly.

'So what about you?' she said. 'What do you look for in a fling?'

'Well, I need to be attracted to her,' he said.

'And?'

'And what? That's it.'

CHAPTER FIVE

GREYSON TYLER didn't strike Charlotte as a particularly cavalier individual. Not when it came to his research. Not when it came to his relationships. He was, however, male—which probably went some way towards explaining his limited thought processes when it came to bedding a woman and walking away.

'Are you attracted to me, Greyson?'

His gaze locked with hers, boldly direct. 'Yes.'

'Do you respect me?'

'Is this another one of your fling criteria?' he murmured.

Charlotte narrowed her gaze.

A hint of a smile tilted Greyson's extremely kissable lips.

'For what it's worth, I have a great deal of respect for the way you conducted yourself at my parents' this afternoon. You did the job I asked of you. You withstood my mother's disapproval with dignity and grace. You were gentle with Sarah. I'm grateful. And I'm impressed.' He set his coffee on the counter, out of harm's way. 'So, do I qualify for a fling? Do I meet your criteria? Because from where I'm standing, I think I do.'

'Modesty's not really one of your strengths,' she murmured.

'No.' Those dark brown eyes lightened a little. 'But then, you didn't specify the need for it.'

'Gilbert was very modest,' she said on a sigh.

'Gilbert was a figment of your imagination,' he reminded her. 'I think you'll find me far more satisfying in any number of ways.'

'You really want to do this?' she murmured.

'Yes.' Not an indecisive bone in this man's superbly sculpted body. 'Do you?'

Did she? Would a night spent in the arms of a man she barely knew chase her loneliness away, even if only for a little while? A man who made her feel warm and protected. One who, for a moment there, back on that deck overlooking the water, made her feel valued and loved. 'Yes.'

His smile came slow and warm. 'As in now?'

'Yes.'

'Noted,' he said silkily. 'But if you don't mind, I might wait a while. What with all this arranging of events, we seem to have lost a bit of spontaneity. I do enjoy spontaneity within lovemaking.'

'You should have said,' she murmured. 'I'd have left the slave bracelets off.'

'Slave bracelets?' His gaze cut to the bracelets at her wrist, and that big body of his became unnaturally still.

'Oh, yes. Did I not mention them? I'm pretty sure I mentioned them to everyone else at the barbecue. The slave bracelets, that is. Signalling possession and worth. A certain willingness to oblige.' Challenge, not submission, and Greyson responded, as Charlotte knew he would, for this man fed on challenge and always would.

He stalked around to her side of the bench and trapped her against it, his hands either side of her on the counter.

Perhaps he'd decided not to take his time after all. Oh, well…

'I'd ask for your thoughts on submission within love-making but I wouldn't want to endanger the spontaneity. So…' She deliberately leaned forward and let her chest brush against his; her nipples responding instantly to all that hardness and heat. He noticed. Charlotte breathed in deeply, savouring the scent of him. He noticed that, too.

'What would you like to do while we wait?' she asked in dulcet tones. 'Would you care for a drink to go with your coffee? Cognac? Brandy liqueur?'

'No.' Greyson's lips were at the spot on her neck, just below the base of her ear where a woman might put perfume only she hadn't worn any perfume. Not today. Next time, if there was such a time, she would apply a scent this man would remember with a deep and abiding pleasure.

He touched the tip of his tongue to her skin next and she gasped her approval, arching her neck to allow him better access. Spontaneity was all well and good but when it came to the act of making love, she far preferred a man who was thorough. One who would not be rushed. One who knew how to take his time.

'Scotch?' she murmured.

'Yes.'

'Now? Or shall I wait for spontaneity to strike?' That earned her a husky rumble that set her hands to his chest and his lips to curving, lips she couldn't help but find with her own. The kiss started out as fleeting and rapidly grew ragged.

'I like it neat, no ice.' Greyson's hands were at her waist. Wide warm palms and long strong fingers, he slid those hands down the sides of her body until he reached her thighs. When he slid his hands back up to her waist he dragged the fabric of her dress with him.

'And the glass?' She closed her eyes and shuddered as the hem of her frock inched higher. 'Square or round?'

'Round.' He lifted her effortlessly and sat her on the bench, stepping in between her legs, forcing them open to accommodate him. The skirt of her dress pooled at her waist. His fingertips slid under it, while his thumbs traced slow circles against the tender flesh of her inner thighs.

'You want that drink now?' she whispered and stifled a gasp as a wayward thumb brushed against the delicate silk of her panties.

'I'm a little busy right now,' he murmured. 'So are you.' His fingers had reached the top of her panties but he didn't try to ease them down her body, not Greyson. He liked his fingers right where they were, with his thumb at her centre, sliding over silk and over nerve endings already swollen and sensitive.

'Aurora would have my hide for being a bad hostess,' she whispered as she covered his wrist with her hand, unsure whether she intended to make him press down deeper or drag his hand away. In the end she did both, one first and then the other as she slid from the countertop, dug an unopened bottle of Scotch from the cupboard, linked fingers with Greyson and led him towards the couch.

Watching Greyson make himself comfortable on the pristine white couch, draping his arms along the back of it and owning the space so utterly, brought a smile to her face.

The swig of Scotch she took straight from the bottle before handing it over brought a smile to his.

He drank his fill and then tilted the bottle towards her. When she shook her head he leaned forward and set the bottle on the low table in front of the couch and reached for her again, drawing her down onto him. She went willingly, straddling his thighs, finding the hard ridge of his arousal and sinking down onto it with a gasp. Plenty to get excited about there. Just *plenty* as his fingers curled into her buttocks and positioned her for best effect.

Arousal bit deep as his lips parted beneath hers, whisky tinged and ravenous as she slid her fingers through his hair and gave herself over to that expert mouth.

Too many clothes and to hell with going slow. One could be both thorough *and* fast, Charlotte decided hastily. Grey's shirt buttons came undone beneath her ministrations. A heartbeat later and the shirt was gone. Beautiful. So very, very beautiful, this man. Charlotte set her hands to his chest and afforded herself the pleasure of dragging them down over rippling muscles until she reached his belt buckle. She made short work of that, and the zipper too, and that which had been encased in denim jutted free.

She rose up onto her knees, rose because she knew exactly what she wanted to do with all that hardness and heat, but her movements put her breasts in line with Greyson's mouth, and he knew what he wanted too. Within the space of a breath he'd eased the spaghetti straps from her shoulders, the silk covering from her breasts, and taken them in his mouth. Such a wicked, teasing mouth. She shuddered against him, straining, whimpering, and he suckled harder and sent a lightning stroke of desire straight to her loins.

His hands were beneath her dress, beneath her panties, testing for slickness and finding it. Only her panties in the way of him now but not for long, one side parting beneath his insistent tug, and then she was sinking down onto him, fast at first and then more slowly as she realised just how much of him she would have to accommodate.

'Easy,' he rumbled against her throat, and then again. 'Easy.' Right before his mouth captured hers for another of those all-consuming kisses.

He didn't rush her. He let her take her time, and if his

breathing came harsh and his hands went to the cushions on either side of him and stayed there, rigidly immobile so as not to hasten her along in any way, it was only to his credit.

'Distract me,' she murmured, fighting her body for every thick and pulsing inch of him. It had been so long for her. She was beginning to doubt her ability to accommodate him.

'You don't need distracting,' he muttered, and brought the fingers of one hand to rest on her abdomen and set his thumb to her centre as he'd done once before. 'You need focus.'

He started off with slow, lazy circles and she focused, heaven help her she did, and slowly, and with infinite patience on his part, she took all of him in.

She stilled his hand, holding onto his wrist with her eyes closed and her lower lip between her teeth as she adjusted to the fullness of him. 'You should come with a warning,' she muttered.

'You should come,' he whispered back, and set about making it happen.

He knew how to move inside a woman slow and easy, this man. He knew how to use the friction of penetration to drive her higher. He knew when to lave and he knew when to bite, and when she came for him and sweet moisture came with it he tumbled her onto her back on the floor and kept her there, his thrusts coming harder now because she wanted them harder, and faster, his every stroke a lesson in ecstasy as she crested around him for the second time in as many minutes.

Grey knew he was a tight fit for a small woman. Holding back was second nature to him, being patient, taking his time—it was the code he lived by, the rule he made love by. But when Charlotte clenched around him again, when her nails dug into his shoulders and she cried out and slammed against him, milking him, coming apart for him, he abandoned all thought of restraint and followed her willingly into madness.

They stayed joined together in the aftermath. Grey rolled to his side and brought Charlotte with him, still buried deep inside her, still trembling. He groaned as she moved but she was only throwing her leg across his hip to keep that connection in place as she eased her upper body back against his outstretched arm.

'I've sworn off lying,' she murmured, and the lazy satisfaction in that velvet voice of hers had his body twitching and threatening to go another round. 'And it's probably not quite the time for teasing either. Maybe later.'

'Is there any particular point to this train of thought?' he queried, and got a not quite accidental elbow in his solar plexus for his efforts.

'Has anyone ever told you you're a very impatient man?'

'No,' he said dryly. 'Never.'

'How unusual.'

'Charlotte,' he said evenly. 'Get to the point.'

'Oh. Right. The point.' She brought her arms above her head and slid him a laughing glance, every bit the wanton gypsy she purported not to be. '*Damn*, that was good.'

Charlotte Greenstone had a God-given talent for understatement, decided Grey upon hearing her words. She also possessed a bone-deep sensuality that he wasn't about to forget in a hurry. One could only hope that in offering him a taste of it, she hadn't taken possession of *him* in the process.

He didn't *feel* as if he'd just met his soul mate.

More as if he'd walked upon a precipice and slipped twenty metres down a hundred-metre cliff and was holding onto his current position by the tips of his bruised and bloodied fingers.

He didn't *think* he was in love with Charlotte.

More like he'd been run over by a truck.

Nothing to worry about though. He'd be up and about again soon. Gone soon enough, as specified by their initial agreement regarding the nature and properties of temporary liaisons.

It occurred to him, fleetingly, that he might want to run.

And then Charlotte slid her hand up and over his chest and around his neck and urged his mouth down to meet hers for a kiss so intensely erotic and full of promise that he immediately fell another twenty metres down that cliff.

'Greyson?' she murmured, and there was absolutely no denying that the sound of his name on her lips was going to haunt him from here to eternity. 'You want to do that again?'

CHAPTER SIX

WAKING up to a sleeping man in her bed wasn't a regular occurrence for Charlotte. She knew his name and she knew where his parents lived. She knew he had a doctorate in botany and that he'd just returned from a three-year research stint in PNG. She knew he made love like a fiend and that she ached in places she'd never ached before. That was about it for what she knew about Greyson Tyler.

It didn't seem enough.

Not for her to have allowed him the liberties she'd allowed him to take with her last night. Not that she remembered a conscious decision to allow him anything once the touching had started.

Spontaneous, that was the word she was looking for. Last night's spontaneous lovemaking had been a revelation. What a woman should *do* with this new information regarding lovemaking and her own hitherto unknown capacity for abandon remained something of a mystery.

She spared a glance for her bed partner. Still sleeping, thank you God, because she could feel a blush coming on just looking at him. He slept on his stomach, with one hand beneath his pillow and the other reaching towards the bed head. He had one knee bent, and he looked for all the world as if he were trying to scale a mountainside.

He seemed to take up an inordinate amount of space in her bed.

Charlotte slipped from the bed and reached silently for her robe. Butt naked was not a regular state of being for her, though she might have to get used to it with this man around. She risked a glance back at him, he was still sleeping so she allowed her gaze to linger on those broad bronzed shoulders and the way the muscles fitted together across his back and tapered down towards his waist. White cotton sheets covered the rest of him, possibly the best of him, but she'd seen it last night and the memory was engraved on her brain.

'Morning,' said a deep and sleepy voice from further up the mountainside and Charlotte dragged her gaze upwards to meet his eyes.

'You're thinking,' he said next.

'No, no, not at all. I think you'll find that I'm just looking.'

'Good,' he said. 'Come here.'

Charlotte raised a sceptical eyebrow.

'Please.'

Much better. She crossed to the empty side of the bed and perched on it, grateful for her breakfast robe, a vivid red silk wrap with a golden dragon embroidered on the back. Kitschy and glorious, and very much her style.

Grey reached up and slid his hand around her neck and drew her down into a kiss that surprised her with its tenderness.

'You okay?' he asked.

'Is this a regular morning-after question for you?'

'Yes.' Long and silky black lashes came down to curtain his eyes as he bussed her lips once more. 'You could try answering it.'

'I'm quite well,' she murmured. 'Possibly even invigo-rated. I'll know more once I've showered.'

Greyson's lashes came up and he regarded her warily. 'I wasn't always easy with you last night.'

'No.' Her turn to initiate the kissing this time. Her choice to linger. 'You weren't. Still…a woman might choose to be grateful for that fact.'

He didn't look reassured. Charlotte stifled a sigh. Perhaps he wasn't as confident in his size and sexuality as she expected him to be. Perhaps he hadn't always… fitted in.

Perhaps a demonstration of her sincerity was in order.

She slid from the bed and headed for the bathroom suite, shedding her robe along the way. Bare butt and a tumble of waist-length tangled black curls—that was the view she afforded him. 'Shower time.' She glanced over her shoulder and offered up a siren's smile. 'It's a big shower.'

She'd been under the spray for only a few minutes before he joined her. Long enough for her to get wet and soapy. Just long enough for her to start wondering if, when she stepped back out of the bathroom, she'd find him gone.

'I'm not normally so careless,' he said gruffly as she turned to face him.

'By careless, do you mean passionate? Fevered? Lost?'

'Yeah, that.'

A woman couldn't help it if her smile turned somewhat smug.

'I usually make a concerted effort to please,' he said next.

'Really?' Now there was a pretty picture. 'Do tell.'

'Why don't I just show you?' he murmured.

Charlotte's smile widened. 'I want you to know that I

really am doing my best to convey to you that last night was an intensely erotic and pleasurable experience for me, with absolutely no apology necessary on your part. Just so we're clear on that point.'

'Consider it clarified,' he said. 'Now turn around to face the tiles.'

'Please.'

He smiled, but he didn't say please. Just turned her gently around and then stepped in behind her and slid his hands down her arms and his fingers over hers before taking her hands and placing her palms against the tiles, shoulder height and body length apart. 'Like this,' he said.

'Please.'

But he didn't say please. Instead, he slid his hands down her body, down to where she was tender and swollen. He parted her legs, caressed her with knowing fingers. 'You okay?'

Did a groan qualify as a yes?

He slid his hands around to her buttocks, filling his palms with them before sliding his hands up the length of her back in one long massaging caress. Arms next, out to her wrists, and then all the way back to where he started.

He kneed her legs open, she braced herself against the wall and stood on tiptoe, waiting for his entry. Expecting it.

'Don't move,' he whispered.

'Don't move, *please*. Alternatively, you could say please don't move. Do you have no manners *at all*?'

'Sometimes, I do,' he countered and there was laughter in that dark, delicious voice. 'I'm very impressed by yours. But just in case you feel obliged to interrupt me any time soon, you can thank me later.'

And then he was kneeling down and wedging broad water-slicked shoulders between her legs and twisting his torso, one strong powerful hand at the small of her back, tilting her pelvis forward, his other hand high on her thigh, as he set his mouth to her centre and feasted.

Charlotte managed to keep her hands to the tiles.

She managed to keep all curses, pleas, and oaths to a minimum.

Later, much later, she remembered to thank him.

Breakfast wasn't a leisurely affair. Charlotte ate grapes from one hand while setting the espresso machine to brewing with the other. She'd dressed for work in her usual working attire—smart trousers, plain shirt, boring shoes—and she'd kept the make-up light, aiming for elegant minimalism. Greyson had shrugged into his clothes of yesterday and followed the creation of Associate Professor Charlotte Greenstone with some bemusement.

'Why the disguise?' he asked finally as she set his coffee in front of him, finished her grapes, and began smoothing back her wayward hair in readiness for a hairclip.

'Who says it's a disguise?' she murmured.

'Seems a little Plain Jane for you,' he said with a shrug. 'Correct me if I'm wrong.'

'I'm a relatively youthful female giving undergraduate lectures and gunning for tenure within an antiquated and patriarchal employment system,' she said with a shrug. 'Respect comes a little easier to some if I look the part.'

'What do you do about the ones who don't respect your abilities, no matter how you dress?'

'They get to learn the hard way.'

Now she'd amused him.

'What?' she snapped. 'Over twenty years of hands-on fieldwork and analysis not enough? Get back in the field, Charlotte, before your godmother's contacts forget you,' she mimicked grimly. 'We wouldn't want you to lose those, now, would we? Or the goodwill that comes with your family name. You are aware, Charlotte, that your ability to pull more funding than the rest of us put together has nothing to do with any actual talent for bringing particular projects and interested parties together? You have a brand name that implies excellent connections, inspired thinking, quality work, and exceptional results, that's all. Don't you be thinking that your success has anything to do with *you*.'

Greyson said nothing.

'You want to know the sad thing about it all?' she said with a frustrated sigh. 'They're not entirely wrong. And now that Aurora's dead, the naysayers are just *waiting* to see how much goodwill towards me died with her.'

'How much goodwill towards you do *you* think died with her?'

'I don't know.' Charlotte wouldn't meet his eyes. 'A lot of these people have known me since I was a baby. They knew my parents. Many of them tutored me in their various areas of expertise. They've followed my career, smoothed the way for me many times over. Because of the brand or because of me or because Aurora called in favours, who knows? I certainly don't. And you really don't need to hear any of this,' she finished with a grimace. 'Sorry. Touchy subject.'

'So who *do* you run all this stuff by?' he asked mildly.

'Well... Gil happened to be a *very* good listener,' she offered, which earned her one of *those* looks.

'Would you like some advice?'

'I'm not sure,' she said warily. 'I might.'

'Don't let anyone tell you that your success is due to

your birthright or a brand you have no influence over. Yes, you had a head start, your upbringing saw to that. But your parents have been dead for, what, twenty years or so? And your godmother was retired for the last five?'

'Something like that,' she murmured.

'And the funding for the projects just keeps coming?' Charlotte nodded.

'Figured as much.' He sipped his coffee. He kept her waiting. Charlotte hated waiting. She had a sneaking suspicion that Greyson knew it. 'The way I see it, Professor, you *are* the brand and have been for some time,' he said at last. 'Your godmother knew it. I dare say she traded on it, added her own to it, taught you how to build it. And you have. Get back out in the field if you want to—if that's where you want to keep your brand based. If you'd rather stay put, all you need do is continue to grow your brand at the management and funding level. It's *your* brand, Charlotte, your life, and you're in the enviable position of being able to choose exactly how you live it. Tell your naysayers to look to their own effectiveness, not yours.'

'You want to know something?' said Charlotte as his words put another chink in her carefully constructed armour.

'I'm not sure,' he offered dryly. 'I might.'

'You're much better at giving advice than Gil.' She glanced at the kitchen clock. 'And I have to get to work. You want to let yourself out? There's a spare set of drive-way keys around here somewhere.'

But to that, he shook his head. 'I'll follow you out.'

'Will you call me?' she asked tentatively. 'Or are we done here?'

Greyson got to his feet. Charlotte adjusted her gaze sky-wards. He looked even bigger than he had last night and a whole lot more lethal. Maybe it was because he hadn't shaved. Maybe she was simply applying her newfound knowledge of how this man thought and what made him tick. What he was capable of giving to a woman by way of encouragement and support. And pleasure.

A shudder ripped through her and it felt like a warning. Just how was she supposed to keep this liaison carefree and temporary when every move he made and word he spoke brought him closer?

'We're not done yet, Charlotte.' Greyson eyed her a little too grimly for comfort. Call it a hunch, but he didn't seem to be embracing their temporary liaison with a whole lot of lightness and joy either. 'You can expect me to call.'

He probably hadn't meant to make it sound like a warning.

Or maybe he had.

'I tried calling you yesterday afternoon to see if you wanted to go to the movies,' said Millie at morning tea time as they raided the biscuit tin for biscuits that weren't a hundred years old. 'Couldn't get through to you though.'

'What did you go and see?'

'I didn't see anything,' said Millie. 'The offer's still open for tomorrow night.'

'Done,' said Charlotte, never mind what films might be playing.

'It's fine if you want to bring someone else along too,' said Millie.

Charlotte shook her head and smiled.

Millie sighed heavily.

'Subtlety will get you nowhere,' said Charlotte archly. 'Ask.'

'Thank you,' said the long suffering Millie. 'What's going on with you and Gil?'

'He's hoping to go and work in Borneo soon. We've

ended our engagement. It was a mutual decision based on many factors.'

'Fool,' muttered Millie. 'Have you seen him lately?'

'I have.'

'Sexy as ever?'

'Alas, yes.'

'Attentive?'

Charlotte felt her face start to heat.

'Feel free to enlighten me,' said Millie. 'Really. I mean it.'

Charlotte smiled again; it was that kind of day. Blue skies above, body sated, mind still trying to work its way through the sensual haze Greyson's lovemaking had left her with. Hard to concentrate on the bigger picture, namely Greyson's—no, *Gil's*—impending exit from her life and from her co-workers' consciousnesses. 'He'll be gone again soon, and that'll be the end of it. Really. It's for the best.'

'What's Borneo got that you haven't?' said Millie.

'Novelty value. Research possibilities. The call of the wild.' Charlotte reeled off the attractions. 'Rainforests. Temples. Orang-utangs.'

'Trifles,' said Mille. 'Though I will confess a fondness for orang-utangs. Have you considered going with him?'

'No,' said Charlotte, and a little bit of brightness went out of her day. 'That's really not an option.'

'Why not? There are opportunities for archaeologists in Borneo. You're wasted here, Charlotte. You know you are. The Mead dangles tenureship in front of you and turns you into his lackey. Carlysle and Steadfellow mine your knowledge and then try and take the credit for it. You could do such brilliant work but you don't. You could tie yourself so lightly to this place and go anywhere. Everywhere.'

'Everywhere's overrated,' said Charlotte lightly, and suffered Millie's puzzled glance.

'I thought it was your godmother's failing health that kept you here,' said Millie. 'But that wasn't it, was it? There's something else. Something bigger than Gil, bigger than love, only I don't know what it is.'

'It's hard to explain,' said Charlotte.

'Try.'

So Charlotte tried. 'I like stability. I like the connections I've made here. I feel like I'm part of something, even when I'm being used up.'

'I still don't get it,' said Millie. Millie, with her big and loving family all around her, brothers and sisters, and parents and cousins, all scattered across a city she knew and loved. Millie didn't know how lucky she was to have that safety net of people who cared for her, people who'd *be* there for each other in times of need.

'Millie—' Charlotte searched for just the right words. Not wanting pity, she'd never wanted that. 'It takes time to get to know a place, to make friends, but I've done that now. Here. And I won't give that up lightly. I feel—I feel that for the first time in my life, I'm starting to belong.'

Grey left it until Friday morning before phoning Charlotte. Never mind that he'd wanted to call her earlier… He hadn't. Self-control had been applied. Restraint. The restraint required of a man embarking on a casual, no-strings affair.

The presence of one Charlotte Greenstone in his life should have made his time between jobs very pleasant. A smart and sensual woman of independent means and a gratifyingly strong sexual appetite wanted to spend a little time with him. Riveting to look at, and with a voice fully capable of coaxing angels downstairs to play in the pit a while—what more could a man *want* from a short-term sexual partner?

A little less perfection of form wouldn't have gone astray, he decided bleakly. She could have at least given the women who were to come after her a fighting chance to measure up.

A little less abandon in the bedroom wouldn't have hurt either, for exactly the same reason.

And would it have killed her to have led a normal life instead of some fascinating life of money, privilege, and discovery? How was a man supposed to do his own work while continually wondering how *hers* was going? The Internet was for instant access to research papers, not for Googling Charlotte's family name to see if he could get a better feel for this *brand* she'd inherited. A glamorous brand, by all accounts. The Greenstones were to archaeology what the Kennedys had been to government. Dazzling, immensely successful and supremely ill-fated. And the only one left was Charlotte.

Who hadn't called.

Or texted.

Or emailed.

Not that he was obsessing. Not that it would do him much good if he were.

He placed the call. Confidence was key. That, and knowing exactly what he wanted from this woman. Right now, he wanted her on *his* turf and he wanted it with an intensity he usually reserved for his work.

'I'm moored at the marina at Hawkesbury River,' he said without preamble when she answered. 'I can offer fresh seafood, cold beer, and a berth on my boat if you've a mind to stay over.'

'Hello, Greyson,' she said, and there was rich amusement in that whisky voice. 'I'd almost given up on hearing from you.'

'I said I'd call.'

'So you did,' she murmured. 'I was hoping you might have managed it a little earlier.'

'You have my number,' he reminded her. 'You could have called me.'

'Ah, but a lady wouldn't,' she murmured. 'Not before you renewed contact and initiated another meeting. Now I can.'

'What particular book of etiquette are you working from?' he said.

'Mine.'

'Don't suppose you have a spare?'

'It's all in my head.'

'That's what I was afraid of. If it's any consolation, I wanted to call you on Monday, Tuesday, and Wednesday, and I almost caved and called you yesterday. There was the small matter of proving to myself that I could wait and work in the interim, not to mention letting you get your own work done.'

'You're very kind.'

'I know. And now it's Friday and the work is done and I'm done with waiting. I want to see you again.'

'Have you heard from Sarah lately?'

'Yes, we've spoken on the phone.' Not a topic he felt inclined to discuss with a woman he wanted in his bed tonight. Even if Charlotte *had* been part of his efforts to deter his former fiancée. 'I've made it brutally clear to both Sarah and my mother that I can't give Sarah what she wants. I've also made it clear to my mother that I was disappointed in her treatment of you.'

'I bet that went down well.'

'It needed to be said. Even with you attending that barbecue with no emotional attachment to me whatsoever, they managed to hurt you. Imagine how much damage they could have done if you *had* had feelings for me.'

'Hence our discussion afterwards about introducing a new partner to Sarah and your family,' said Charlotte. 'I'm glad you took those thoughts on board, Greyson,' she said softly. 'To be honest, I didn't expect you to take them on board on *my* account. They were intended for the women who came after me.'

'What? You don't think you deserve to be treated with respect or given a fair go?'

Grey waited for some wry and clever comeback but Charlotte stayed strangely silent.

'My mother wants to know my intentions towards you.'

'What did you tell her?' Wariness in Charlotte's beautiful velvet voice now. A reserve he didn't want to hear.

'I told her I'd never met a more fascinating woman.' Truth. Bare and unvarnished and Charlotte could make of it what she would. 'I wasn't lying, Charlotte. I want to see you again. Have dinner with me tonight. Stay over if you like or head home afterwards but come. Come spend some time with me.'

'Okay.' Nothing cool about Charlotte now. Her voice had gone husky, bringing with it memories of whispered entreaties and outrageous sexual pleasure. 'I figure I can be there around seven. And Greyson?'

'What?'

'Thank you for championing me, and, yes. I'm of a mind to stay over.'

Charlotte's commute home from work took time. The drive down to the Hawkesbury involved getting across the bridge and through the city during Friday night rush hour, and took considerably longer. She'd called Greyson to inform him of her delay in case it affected the dinner plans. He'd assured her it wouldn't. He'd told her to take her time. She'd told him he'd better be worth it. Not his decision to make, he'd told her, and hung up.

One slow and crooked smile of welcome from Greyson as he took her overnight bag from her and held out his hand to help her up the stairs of his gleaming catamaran went some way towards making Charlotte glad she'd said yes to his plans. The way he filled out his grey canvas long shorts and had left his white shirt unbuttoned went further.

'In my defence, I'd forgotten all about the traffic,' he said, and mollified her some more.

'So had I,' she said as she slipped off her shoes to go barefoot on his deck. A very high deck, she decided as she straightened and glanced over the side of the catamaran. 'Nice boat. I should have realised you'd be a sailor, what with your folks' holiday house on the water and your water-weed work.'

'I was five when I got my first catamaran,' he said affably as he guided her along the craft towards an enclosed area that spanned the twin hulls. 'It was love at first sight. I wanted to sleep on it. My mother said I could when I got a bit older.'

'How old were you before you got your way?'

'Eight.' No sign of the formidable Dr Greyson Tyler in the grin he shot her; he was all boy and finally living his dream. 'Longest three years of my life.'

Greyson opened a sliding glass door into a spacious living area, compact galley with plenty of bench space and sitting areas to one side, a lounge area to the other and more seats and a table to the fore. 'I usually eat in here,' he said. 'Sleeping quarters are down in the hulls.' He set Charlotte's bag at her feet and his smile turned wry. 'Guest hull is to your left, mine's to your right, and I've no idea what etiquette demands. You choose.'

'Where do your women friends usually sleep?'

'Not here,' he said gruffly and continued with the tour. 'Bridge is above us and there's a little cove where we can anchor for the night about fifteen minutes away. Your call which comes first, food or more travel. There's a plate of seafood starters in the fridge. We can take it up to the bridge if you're inclined to multitask.'

'You eat on the bridge?'

'I do when it's past dinner time and I want to appease a beautiful woman,' he murmured. 'I can be flexible.'

'And I can be grateful,' she said. 'I'm for getting under way and I'll bring the feast to you.'

Greyson nodded and headed back along the cat, casting off and heading for the bridge. They weren't under sail and moments later an engine purred to life. Charlotte made herself at home in the little galley, opening the fridge and pulling out a high-lipped flat-bottomed bowl crammed with shelled king prawns, oysters, and various types of dipping sauce.

Not a dish that required hours of fiddly preparation, but effort had been made nonetheless. Point for Greyson.

Dish in hand, Charlotte headed out of the cabin and climbed the stairs to the bridge as Greyson eased the craft slowly away from the dock. Once clear of the marina and other craft, he throttled up and the cat responded with surprising alacrity. Plenty of horsepower at Greyson's fingertips, and as for the catamaran itself, a great deal more luxury than Charlotte had expected. This wasn't just a pleasure craft; it was a home, and one that reflected the wanderlust of its owner.

Charlotte reached Greyson's side and smiled at the dark eyed devil who greeted her with a swift and potent smile of his own.

Terrible fiancé material, this man—as the patient, still-smitten Sarah had discovered.

But on a night like this, for an outing of this nature, he was damn near perfect.

They motored past the small township of Hawkesbury River, past tree clad ridges rising up from the riverbanks. They motored under an old railway bridge and on to where solitude and natural beauty held sway.

The catamaran rode high in the water, and looking out over the wide expanse of glassy river held plenty of appeal. Leaning back against the instrument panel and watching Greyson's eyes darken as she fed him a prawn held more. From her hand to his lips, and if feeding him took on a savagely sensual edge, well, it was only to be expected in such a setting and with such a man.

'Tell me about your work,' she said.

'What would you like to know?'

'What inspires you the most. What a regular day is like for you. Where you think your research will lead. Just the usual.'

He took an oyster on the half shell from her outstretched hand. 'That's not the usual.'

'It's not?' Charlotte briefly wondered what *was* the usual, and what type of woman Greyson would normally choose to spend time with. Sarah hadn't been a shallow woman by any stretch of the imagination and Greyson's mother had been downright formidable. Perhaps his taste ran more to sweetly obliging types these days. 'Sorry.'

Greyson devoured the oyster and set the shell to the side of the plate where Charlotte had been neatly stacking them. 'I like the element of discovery that comes with the research,' he said at last. 'I like exploring the applications that stem from such a discovery.'

'Ever think of being an archaeologist?' she asked dryly.

'I prefer the living world,' he murmured. 'Ancient cities can be dazzling but they aren't my passion. Plant interactions are.'

'And then there's the travel,' she said.

'Exactly. As for a regular day, it varies. At the moment I'm here on the boat, sitting in front of a laptop for most of the day, running the stats on experimental results. It's data entry at its most pedestrian—until you find something. And I never know what I'll find until I find it, or where it will lead until I get there. That's the beauty of it.'

'A man who savours the journey.'

'Don't you?' he countered.

'I used to.' Charlotte stared past him, out over the water and the increasingly dusky sky. 'And then somewhere in my mid twenties I started wondering what it might be like to stay in one place for a while. So instead of scraping away at how other people lived, I took the Sydney uni job and tried to put something of what all those ancient civilisations had taught me into practice.'

'What did they teach you?'

'That sooner or later everyone needs a home. An environment they can control. A place to retreat to. Somewhere that brings them peace.'

'And does your apartment by the bridge feel like a home?' he asked quietly.

'I've been asking myself the same question for a while now.' Charlotte shrugged and looked out over the water. 'Sooner or later I'm going to have to decide what to do about Aurora's house. I really don't need two.'

'Which one's closer to your workplace?'

'The apartment. But Aurora's has more sentimental value. It's the closest thing to a childhood home that I've got. We used to make a point of going back there at least once a year.'

'For how long?'

'A couple of weeks,' said Charlotte. 'A month if I was lucky.'

'What about school?' asked Greyson.

'We used the New South Wales distance education system,' said Charlotte. 'Tailored for children who travelled, children who roamed. Aurora supplemented it, of course. She had a knack for making the past come alive so the histories fast became our passion. I studied the Battle of Waterloo by walking the battlefield. I sat in the Colosseum and dreamed of gladiators and the roar of a Roman crowd.'

'It sounds idyllic.'

'It was richly rewarding,' said Charlotte quietly. 'And sometimes it was incredibly lonely. It's why I resist the notion of taking the archaeology road again. At least here I have friends and a place that's mine.'

'Two places, in fact,' murmured Greyson dryly.

'Exactly.' Charlotte fed him another prawn. 'I like *your* home, by the way. It's very you.'

'Thank you. We're almost at the cove.'

And then they *were* at the cove and Greyson was cutting the engine and dropping anchor as the last shards of light from a long gone sun surrendered to the night.

Charlotte smiled and let Greyson take the near empty food tray and lead her inside. He fetched some drinks—a white wine for her, beer for himself. He took two cheese-sauce-covered lobster halves from the fridge and shoved them in the oven. He looked comfortable in the kitchen. At home.

Charlotte had never once pictured Gil in the kitchen. Certainly not in a ship's galley. Nor had Gil ever been quite so delectably dressed.

'You're smiling,' Grey murmured.

'I know.' She set her wine on the bench and flowed into Greyson's arms, burrowing beneath his open shirt in search of warm skin over rippling muscle. She touched the tip of her tongue to his collarbone and tasted salt. He put his hand to her head and held her there for a moment, breathing in deep, before tilting her head back and covering her lips with his own in a kiss that spoke of welcome, and wanting, and a man who intended to savour every moment of this particular journey.

'Miss me?' he whispered, between kisses.

'It's really not part of the plan,' she countered and kissed him again. She didn't tell him that sinking into his kisses felt a lot like coming home. She didn't say that she'd thought about him far more than she'd wanted to this past week. That she'd envied him his overprotective mother and his lovely ex-fiancée, the work that was his passion, and the surety with which he moved through life. A smart and sexy man who knew exactly what he wanted was a very attractive proposition for a woman who did not.

He filled a gap, as Gil had filled a gap. He fed a need Charlotte hadn't known existed.

'I think I'm using you,' she murmured.

'That's okay.' He kissed her again. This time she moaned her approval. 'Blame it on the endorphins.'

'You don't recommend that I take at least *some* responsibility for my behaviour?'

'We have a short-term liaison agreement, remember? Your behaviour is entirely appropriate. You could even—just a suggestion—increase your enthusiasm for my company.'

'You called, I came,' she countered, stepping out of his embrace and retrieving her wine. 'Undress me, make love to me, and I guarantee I'll come some more. How much more enthusiasm do you want?'

'Maybe enthusiasm wasn't quite the right word,' Greyson said smoothly. 'Never mind.'

He reached for his beer, leaned back against the tiny galley sink, and studied her intently. 'My mother phoned this evening to ask me what I was doing this weekend. I told her I was spending it with you. She wants you over for dinner again, some time. Just the four of us, my father included.'

'Why?' asked Charlotte warily.

'Perhaps she feels that she didn't give you a chance.'

'She doesn't have to.'

'Alas, she doesn't know that.' Grey studied her some more. 'I'll tell her you're busy.'

Charlotte lowered her gaze. Had she really been in-volved with Greyson, she'd have grasped the olive branch extended. As it was...he could tell his mother whatever he liked.

'It's one of the drawbacks of having a nosey family,' he said next. 'My mother's been after grandchildren for years.'

'Grandchildren?'

'What's your position on that?' he asked and Charlotte glanced back towards him to find his gaze more intent than ever.

'On grandchildren?' she said lightly. 'I can see the appeal.'

'On children,' he said. 'And you having them.'

'Yours?'

'Anyone's.'

'Again, I can see the appeal,' she said. 'And were I in a loving and stable relationship, I might consider children an option.'

'What if your partner had a vocation that required travel? Would you consider joining him on his travels? You and the children?'

'Are we talking about a partner much like yourself?'

'Let's assume yes,' he said.

'It's not a question I've given much thought to,' she said. 'Mainly because the plan is to avoid becoming involved with such a man. I've a lot of experience when it comes to unorthodox childhoods, Greyson. I know what worked for me, and what didn't. I'll not be repeating what didn't.'

'Wouldn't that make you the perfect partner for such a man?' he said silkily.

'That would depend on his ability to forfeit his needs and desires for the greater good of his family when the time came for him to do so,' she said, equally silkily. 'Could *you*?'

'Good question,' he said blandly and peeked into the oven. 'I think they're done.'

They ate on deck, bypassing the perfectly prepared table in favour of a starry sky, a playful breeze, and balancing their plates on their knees. It fed Greyson's need for freedom and Charlotte's need for escape from difficult questions and impossible compromises. When they were done with the food she relaxed back against the moulded bench seating and stared at the sky. You couldn't see the stars from where she was in Sydney. Not many, at any rate, and not often. 'I'm not *against* travel,' she murmured. 'I'm very fond of new horizons and experiences.'

'I see that,' he murmured.

'Just not as an ongoing way of life.'

'Have you ever made love beneath the stars?' he murmured.

'Are you changing the subject?'

'Yes,' he said. 'I've had enough of the old subject. I'm hunting a new one. Have you ever made love outside, under the stars?'

'No.'

'Want to?'

She rose and straddled him, pushing his shirt from his shoulders as she'd wanted to do all evening, glorying in his size and his strength and the lazy intensity he could bring to a moment. 'Yes,' she said. 'I do.'

He didn't mean to devour her. He hadn't meant to bring up his mother's dinner invitation or the subject of children either. Hadn't meant to make love to her half the night and then again come sunrise because he couldn't get enough of her. But he did all those things to Charlotte Greenstone and she matched him, passion for passion, and warned him that last time, before her eyes had fluttered closed, that if he didn't want her committing mutiny, her breakfast had better be bountiful and could he please serve it some time after ten.

'What did your last Sherpa die of?' he'd muttered.

'Boredom,' she'd mumbled and promptly fallen asleep.

Greyson wasn't bored.

Exasperated, at times. Astonished by the sexual plea- sure he found in Charlotte's embrace. But not bored.

He had a plan, formulated last night in between one bout of lovemaking and the next. A stupid plan, half baked and wholly crazy and one he wasn't at all sure he'd be able to sell to Charlotte as a viable option, given her soul deep aversion to traipsing around the globe according to someone else's whim. Still, he did have a habit of getting what he wanted. Eventually.

Grey waited until ten-thirty to wake Charlotte from her slumber. He used a mug of the finest highland coffee PNG had to offer to rouse her. He told her the pancakes would be ready by eleven, and that there were fresh towels and toiletries in the bathroom. He thought he heard the words *slave driver* mumbled by way of reply, along with a few other odd words like *incubus*, *sadist*, and *dead man*.

Perhaps she'd been comparing him favourably to Gil.

'I have a plan,' he said when Charlotte was wholly awake and halfway through her pancakes and coffee. 'Will you hear me out?'

'Does it involve your mother?'

'No, although I dare say she'll have something to say about the matter. It involves me going to Borneo next week to scout locations for the new project. And you coming with me.'

Charlotte chewed slowly and swallowed hard. She reached for her coffee, deliberately stalling for time. Grey kept his mouth shut and let her stall. Press her and he'd lose her. Rush her and she'd bolt. Challenge her and he might just be able to persuade her around to his way of thinking.

'Why would I do that?' she said finally.

'Because it'd give you an opportunity to test your feelings about travel,' he offered. 'You'll get all the vagaries of working a remote location without having to involve your own work. Then if the lifestyle still holds no appeal for you, your work will be exactly how and where you left it. Face it, Charlotte. You're a little hazy right now when it comes to the direction you want your career to take. A trip like this can't hurt and might even help clarify your thoughts on the matter.'

She didn't deny it. 'What's in it for you?' she asked warily.

'You mean apart from the insanely good sex?'

He won a tiny smile from her. 'You have a one-track mind.'

'So I've been told. Usually by people who fail to comprehend the bigger picture.' He sent her his most reassuring smile, not particularly wanting to discuss his big-picture plans with her at the moment. 'I'll pay your way, of course.'

Just like that, her smile disappeared. 'Don't be daft.'

'Why is that daft? My invite, my expense. Your rules, remember?'

'Those rules aren't applicable to this situation.'

'My mistake,' he said smoothly. 'You presented your position on the matter of who pays for what strongly enough that I naturally assumed there was no room for movement. You present your position on careers that require extensive travel with equal conviction, but again, I sense uncertainty as to *why* you consider them not to your liking. I leave on Wednesday. Sydney to mainland Malaysia, then a couple of regional flights to get to a little river city called Banjarmasin.'

'I know it,' she said flatly.

'I've an interest in the conservation forests there.'

Charlotte picked up her fork and cut into her pancake with the edge of it, deftly liberating a chunk before stabbing it with the end of her fork. She put it to her mouth, chewed, swallowed, and smiled. 'I'm sure there'll be plenty there to interest you.'

'And to interest you?'

'Well, the monkeys are very sweet,' she murmured. 'When do you need my answer by?'

'No rush. Although some time before Wednesday,

obviously.' He sipped his coffee. 'Anywhere you need to be today?'

'Not really. I often spend Sunday afternoon at Aurora's house. It appeases the neighbours.'

'If I dropped you back at the marina tomorrow morning, you could be there by lunchtime. Would that work?'

'I didn't bring two days' worth of clothes.'

'Wear mine.'

'Are you asking me to sleep over again tonight?'

'Yes.'

'So you can convince me to come traipsing with you?'

'Because I'm enjoying your company and I'm not quite ready to let you go.' He gave her the truth of his thoughts in that he gave her what he thought she would bear. 'A short term affair doesn't by nature have to lack intensity.'

'So I'm discovering,' she murmured.

'Will you stay on another night?'

'Will you try and convince me to come travelling with you next week if I do?'

'No.' Greyson shook his head. 'My offer stands but I'll not badger you into accepting it. That's not my way. I'm quite happy to leave the question hanging there if you are.'

'The old elephant in the living room,' she said with a wry smile.

'Exactly.'

'So what would we do with the day if I stayed on?' she said at last, and watched Greyson's eyes lighten and brighten with possibilities.

'Wind's picking up,' he said. 'Have you ever raced a cat under sail?'

* * *

They raced the day away and made the most of the night.

Greyson kept his word. He never once mentioned his offer. Instead he made love to her with a focus no other man had ever matched. Passion ruled him, ruled them both, along with greedy abandon in Charlotte's case, liberally laced with desperation at the thought that this night might be their last.

Morning came too soon for Charlotte but she savoured it regardless, delighting in being wooed awake by wicked promises and exceptionally good coffee. A woman could get used to such treatment, but only a foolish woman would allow herself to depend on it.

She'd thought about joining Greyson in Borneo for the week. One week, what harm could it do? She had holiday time owing. Time her boss had urged her to take. She had no commitments to pets or to people—no responsibilities at all in that regard. She was a free agent and why shouldn't she follow her heart—or at least her libido for a time—and see where it led?

Tempting, so tempting, this man's kisses, as she and Greyson stood on dry land later in the day, saying their farewells beside her baking hot car, and stealing kisses where they could. Charlotte stole a lot of them, a woman bent on gorging herself before a famine.

'Safe travels, Greyson Tyler,' she murmured, and if her heart felt as if it was breaking, well, perhaps it was. She stood back and took one last look at him, storing up the memories for later. A big beautiful man with tousled black hair, intelligent brown eyes, more charm than was good for him, and an air of command and purpose that clung to him like skin. 'I'll think of you with pleasure and I'll think of you with regret, but I'll not be going with you to Borneo.'

'Why not?' His turn to move forward, to reach for her and coax every last drop of pleasure from a kiss. 'We're good together, Charlotte. Better than good.'

'I know. And maybe in another lifetime, one shaped by a different upbringing, I'd have followed you and never looked back.' She stepped back, out of his arms and the solace she found there and regarded him pensively. 'You think I don't know my own mind or that you can change it. Somewhere along the way, I've given you the impression that I don't know what I want from a partner or from this life, and maybe I don't. Not fully, not with certainty. Thing is, no matter how often I examine the notion of travel or of being with a partner who travels, there's a resistance there that runs soul deep.'

'Call me,' he said gruffly. 'When I get back.'

'Greyson.' She looked away, down at the suddenly blurry steering wheel of her car, anywhere but at him. How had she come to care for him so much in such a short time? Two weeks. Less than half a dozen meetings, and already he was tearing her in two. 'I can't.' Nothing more than a ragged plea for mercy, for he seemed bent on making this farewell so much harder than it should have been. 'I can't,' she whispered again.

'Then I'll call you.'

'Greyson, please…' She pressed her lips to his, one final farewell. She stepped back and smiled through her tears. Time to go before she begged him to stay. 'Don't.'

CHAPTER SEVEN

GREYSON TYLER wasn't always an easy man to deal with. He had his fair share of dogged determination. He knew exactly how well persistence paid off. He hadn't wanted to walk away from Charlotte Greenstone when she'd asked him to. His body had screamed no and his brain had assured him that he could overcome her protests eventually. Only honour had stayed his hand.

Charlotte hadn't refused him in haste—she'd thought about his offer, thought hard about where their fledgling relationship might lead and what he could give her that she wanted. Her conclusion had been a valid one.

Not enough.

He'd heard that tune before. He knew all the words.

This time round, they hammered home hard.

He went to Borneo. He stayed the week and decided he had all the skills required to do good work there—if he had a mind to. Living conditions would be perfectly adequate. The seafood was exceptional. He'd be on the water a lot, and that always endeared a project to him, for the water was his home. He knew of half a dozen funding opportunities coming up. He should have been busy writing and sending out proposals.

And yet…a week passed, and then another three, and

he still hadn't written an outline for what he wanted to do in Borneo.

He tried telling himself it was because the PNG data had proved so richly rewarding, and he'd been distracted by that, and by all the research papers to be had from it. He even wrote some of those papers and was pleased with his efforts. Dr Grey Tyler was doing good work—work that, when reviewed and published, should make finding grant money for future projects easy.

Six months was all he'd allowed himself when it came to mining the PNG data for papers and two of those had already passed. He needed to get another project in place soon or he'd be out of work.

Being out of work held no appeal whatsoever.

Neither, he finally admitted to himself, did spending the next three years in a tiny fishing village in Borneo.

Something else, then. Something fascinating and captivating and a little more civilised would surely command his attention sooner or later.

And he wasn't talking about Charlotte Greenstone.

With Greyson—and Gilbert—out of the picture, Charlotte attempted to settle back into her normal routine with joy, and, if not joy, then at least some measure of contentment. Alas, embracing her inner contentment really wasn't going so well.

Restlessness plagued her. She couldn't settle to her work.

For the first time in five years, the congestion of inner city Sydney got on her nerves, and the charm of her nose-to-girder view of the Harbour Bridge, and the vibrations that shook the windows with every passing passenger train, wore thin.

Life didn't shine so brightly these days. Emptiness had

crept back into her life and this time it stayed. Dreariness and weariness had crept in too—ugly unwanted companions that she couldn't seem to shake.

Crankiness… Heaven help her, she had a short fuse these days.

The Mead had requested a meeting this morning to discuss a dig he was keen to find funding for. No guesses required as to whose job that would be. Following that, she had two undergraduate lectures scheduled for ten and twelve, and a doctor's appointment to go to in the afternoon.

It was seven a.m. and all Charlotte wanted to do was crawl back into bed and relive a morning or two when she'd woken up in a strong and loving man's arms and been treated to coffee in bed and pancakes with syrup, and a day of sailing and sunshine that she'd never wanted to end.

'Damn you!' she muttered to the man who'd given her that day. *'A curse on you, Greyson Tyler.'* A really good curse, for having the temerity and the God-given *attributes* to worm his way into her psyche and stay there.

Greyson the gone—be he in Borneo, PNG, roasting over hot coals…wherever.

Gone.

Charlotte's meeting with Harold Mead didn't start well. She was ten minutes late, the smell of the coffee he handed her made her want to throw up, and there were two other suits in the room—one of them the head of university finance, the other one the Dean of Geology. She smelled collaboration and coercion and they came through on that in spades. A joint dig involving every geologist, archaeologist, and currently aimless dogsbody on the payroll of three different universities. Charlotte would not be in charge, of course. She wouldn't even be required to step foot on site, if that was her preference. Nor would they utilise her field expertise, nor, by extrapolation, did they intend to credit her with any of the research.

No, Charlotte's sole task was to shake the loose change from the private sector in order to fund the project.

She declined. Politely.

She damn near resigned. Not so politely.

'Charlotte, I don't know what to do with you,' Harold Mead told her after the other two had left, his frustration and disappointment clearly evident. 'You won't commit to any field work, you pick and choose which projects you'll support with no clear research direction that I can discern, you *say* you'd like to move into project set-up and administration and yet here I am offering that to you on a plate and you refuse. What exactly is it that you *want*?'

'How about we start with some small level of *input* into the projects the Greenstone name is expected to sell,' she countered hotly, knowing her words were unprofessional but powerless to stop them tumbling out. 'An assurance that my experience might, at some stage, be *valued* when it comes to modifying a project plan, and not swept aside because I'm young and female and couldn't possibly know better than you.'

'Sometimes you don't,' said the Mead curtly.

'And sometimes I *do*,' she said. 'You want to know what I *want*? Fine. I'll have a proposal on your desk tomorrow morning, outlining my thoughts on project funding and administration in detail. I suggest you look it over rather closely, see if you can bring yourself to accommodate at least *some* of my suggestions, because if not I'll be moving on and taking my family name and my cashed-up connections with me.'

Two lectures, a salad sandwich, and a hasty drive

through the city centre later, Charlotte arrived at the Circular Quay surgery near her apartment. Twenty minutes after she took a seat in the waiting room, the doctor called her in.

The affable doctor Christina Christensen sat her down, looked her over and asked her what was wrong. 'Lethargy, loss of appetite, and a tendency to get a wee bit emotional over the strangest things,' she said.

'What kind of things?' the doctor asked as she reached for the blood pressure bandage.

'Well...this morning I was howling along to a piece of music,' said Charlotte.

'It happens,' said the doctor. 'You should see me at the opera.'

'It wasn't that kind of music.'

'What kind was it?' asked the doctor.

'Beethoven's Ninth. Seriously, I'm getting more and more irrational of late. Short-tempered. Opinionated.'

'Anything else?'

'Cross,' said Charlotte.

'You already said that.'

'It probably bears repeating.'

'Tell me about your appetite,' said the doctor as she pumped up the pressure wrap around Charlotte's upper arm to the point of pain and then abruptly released the pressure.

'What's to tell? It's gone.'

'Any uncommonly stressful events surrounding you lately?'

'That would be a yes,' muttered Charlotte. 'But I'm either getting on top of them or coming to terms with them.'

'Lucky you,' said the doctor. 'Your blood pressure's fine. How much weight have you lost?'

'A couple of kilos in the past couple of weeks.'

'Scales are over there,' said the doctor.

And when Charlotte stepped on them and the readout settled, 'You're a little lean, but nothing to worry about. Periods regular?'

'I'm on the pill,' muttered Charlotte. 'I went on them *because* of irregular periods.'

'Any chance you could be pregnant?' asked the doctor, gesturing for Charlotte to return to the patient's chair.

Charlotte didn't answer her straight away. She was too busy counting back time and fighting terror.

The doctor opened a desk drawer and pulled out a box full of little white individually wrapped plastic sticks. She set one on the desk in front of Charlotte. 'Ever used one of these?'

'No.' *Hell*, no.

'Bathroom's two doors down. Pee on the window end, shake off the excess moisture, and bring it back here.'

'I really don't thin—'

'Go,' said the doctor gently. 'If it comes up negative, I'll order you some blood tests to see if there's another reason for the changes you're describing, but first things first.'

Right. First things first. Nothing to panic about.

Charlotte held to the 'first things first' motto all through the long walk to the bathroom and through the business with the pregnancy-kit stick. A blue line already ran across the window of the stick—that was good, right? It was the crosses you had to worry about.

'Just pop it on the paper towel there,' said the good doctor when Charlotte returned. 'It'll only take a couple of minutes.'

Longest two minutes of Charlotte's life.

The doctor chatted. Inputted data into Charlotte's patient file. Asked her if she was currently in a steady relationship and whether she'd been considering mother-hood, of late.

'No,' said Charlotte, and, 'No.' While another little line grew slowly stronger and transacted the first.

Eventually the doctor looked down and then back up at Charlotte, her gaze sympathetic. 'We can do it again,' she said. 'We can take a blood test to confirm, but I think you'd best brace yourself for unexpected news.' The doctor's smile turned wry. 'Congratulations, Ms Greenstone. You're pregnant.'

Charlotte sat unmoving, her gaze not leaving that terrible little stick.

'I want to see you again in a few days' time,' continued the doctor. 'We'll talk more then. About options. What happens next. Until then, take it easy, don't skip meals, and be kind to yourself.' The doctor studied her intently. 'Do you have anyone you can talk to about this? Family? Friends? The father?'

Charlotte didn't answer straight away. Mainly because her gut response had been no. There was no one to talk to or turn to. No one at all.

'Charlotte, do I need to refer you to a counsellor?' Dr Christina Christensen's eyes were kind and knowing. She'd probably seen this response before. 'I can pull some strings and get you in to see one this afternoon, if need be.'

What was the doctor saying now? Something about a counsellor? Charlotte stared at her uncomprehendingly. She had no words. There were no words for this.

'Charlotte.' The doctor's voice was infinitely gentle. 'I'm going to make an appointment for you to talk to a family counsellor this afternoon.'

'No!' Another emotional outburst in a morning filled with them. 'No,' she repeated more calmly. 'I'm fine.' Not shattered, or terrified beyond belief. 'Pregnant, right? But otherwise fine.'

The doctor sat back in her chair and steepled her fingers, her gaze not leaving Charlotte's face.

'I have people I can talk to,' said Charlotte next. 'I do.' Imaginary Aurora. Back from the dead, fictional ex-fiancé Gil.

'Your call on the counsellor,' said the doctor. 'But I still want to see you in three days' time. Make the appointment on your way out.'

Charlotte made the appointment and made it to her car. She didn't make it home to her apartment. Instead she drove to Aurora's and went to the kitchen and made herself a cup of tea, black because there was no milk in the house because she'd cleaned out and turned off the fridge, and sugared, because there was sugar in the cupboard and sugar was good for shock. She sat in Aurora's conservatory-style kitchen and stared out over the gardens to the harbour beyond and tentatively tried picking her way through her chaotic emotions.

A baby. Dear God, a baby to love and to care for. Loneliness in exchange for motherhood. A child to teach. A child who would learn what she had learned, what everyone learned eventually. That life was glorious and unexpected and too often brutal. A child who had no one. No one but her.

Only that wasn't quite true, for this was Greyson's child too.

Greyson the magnificent, with his loving family and his travelling life.

What now? What on earth was she supposed to do now?

I miss you, Aurora. I wish you were here. I wish…

A memory started forming; a vivid picture in her mind.

A lamp-lit private library and an overstuffed leather armchair. Aurora in her thirties and Charlotte at five. A leather bound children's picture book rich with story and life. Aurora's fine voice; such a marvellous sound.

If wishes were horses then beggars would ride...

Drawing her knees up to her chest, Charlotte wrapped her arms tightly around herself, and wept.

'You need to be at work,' said Millie two days later, while sitting in Charlotte's sunny apartment kitchen beneath the bridge. The bridge still loomed large and the windows still shook when the trains went by, but those things had ceased to annoy her. These days Charlotte was all about simply being grateful that she owned her own homes, that she didn't need to work to support herself, and that when it came to the things that money could buy, neither she nor this baby would ever go without.

Reason had returned to Charlotte, or, if not reason exactly, at least a functioning awareness of how fortunate she was. She had an education and a great deal of wealth. She had stability and a good life.

She even had friends who cared enough to call in on their way home from work, seeing as Charlotte *hadn't* been in to work these past few days. Millie was here, bearing flowers and cake, and Charlotte was ridiculously glad of her company. Grateful that Millie had thought enough of their friendship to drop by. Glad that Millie brought with her gossip from work.

Charlotte had almost tendered her resignation the afternoon she'd received news of her impending motherhood but she'd dredged up a thimbleful of professionalism from somewhere and put together a 'Greenstone Foundation' proposal instead and emailed it off to the Mead.

A proposal that—the more she thought about it—didn't

really require the university's participation at all. One that outlined her preferred project set-up, co-ordination, collaboration, and financing practices. One that granted the university beneficial ties to the foundation and in return requested that the university provide her with a management assistant. Preferably one eager to travel with or without her to dig sites in order to oversee operations. Preferably one who'd worked outside the academic arena and had real world skills in place as well as the necessary archaeology qualifications. Preferably Derek.

'Seriously, Charlotte,' said Millie, from her spot at the kitchen counter, where she'd taken to slicing up the walnut loaf she'd brought with her, 'the entire department's in an uproar about this foundation of yours and what's in it for them—Derek loves the idea, by the way—but you not being around to explain your vision isn't helping any. You need to get in there and get forceful if you want it to happen.'

'I want it to happen,' said Charlotte simply.

'So you'll be back at work on Monday?'

Charlotte nodded. 'You want some coffee to go with your walnut slice?'

Millie nodded.

Charlotte set the coffee maker to gurgling. She headed for the fridge. Out came the milk for the coffee and double dollop cream for the cake.

'So what prompted this Greenstone Foundation idea?' asked Millie.

'Aurora's death,' said Charlotte. 'More money than I know what to do with. The need for a challenge. Not getting the leeway or the recognition I wanted from the university employment system. Take your pick. Life lacked purpose. The foundation will give me one. And flexibility as well. Happens I'm going to need that too.'

'What does Gil think of your newfound purpose?' asked Millie.

'I've no idea.'

'Ah.' Millie's eyes turned sympathetic. 'Guess you two didn't sort out your differences, then.'

'No. Some people never lose the wanderlust. Grey's one of them.'

'Who's Grey?'

'Gil,' said Charlotte. 'Thaddeus. Only he's not Thaddeus either. He's Greyson.'

'The man has more names than a birth registry,' muttered Millie, and bit into her now cream-slathered walnut slice.

Charlotte smiled and toyed with her own food. 'So it seems.' What to tell and what to withhold from a woman whose friendship she'd come to value? 'Millie, will you keep a confidence for me?'

'Is it likely to impact negatively on my work, my relationship with others, or my ethics?' asked Millie.

'Not really,' said Charlotte. 'Maybe a little. It's probably not going to do a whole lot for your opinion of me.'

Millie put down her slice, wiped her hands on the napkin, sipped her coffee, and set it down gently. First things first. 'Okay,' she said cautiously. 'What's up?'

'Gil Tyler was a figment of my imagination. Grey Tyler is the man who came to collect his office. They're not one and the same. And I haven't finished yet.'

Harder than she'd thought, this unburdening of her sins. So many, *many* lies. It was time for them to stop.

'Okay.' Millie's eyebrows had risen considerably. 'Continue.'

'Grey and I slept together a time or two. It was…intense. Amazing. But strictly short term. We parted ways relatively amicably.'

It seemed as good a summary as any, even if it did downplay the intensity of the real thing.

'Sounds like a good time was had by all,' said Millie.

'And now I'm pregnant.'

Millie blinked, nodded slowly, and kept her mouth firmly shut.

'Not deliberately,' said Charlotte hastily. 'This would be one of those extremely unexpected pregnancies. As opposed to a planned one.'

Another slow nod from Millie.

'Millie, say something.'

'Yes,' said Millie. 'Yes, I believe that *is* the custom. I just need a moment's processing time. And we're definitely going to need more cake.'

'I have mountains of cake,' said Charlotte. 'Also ice cream, pickles, and caramel tart, just in case. All I'm after is your uninhibited response to my news.'

Millie sent her a speaking glance.

'Although any response will do.'

'Does anyone else know?' asked Millie.

'Not yet. You're my practice run.'

'Oh, the pressure to say something you might actually want to hear,' murmured Millie. 'I feel like I'm on a game show and you're the host, waiting for my reply to the million dollar question.' Millie put both hands to her head and groaned. 'Can I phone a friend?'

'Who?'

'Derek.'

'Only if you're planning on inviting him over,' said Charlotte. 'I may need him for my second practice run. I think I've blown the first.'

Millie ran her hands over her hair and looked back up at Charlotte, her eyes imploring. 'I don't know what to say.'

'Say I can do this,' pleaded Charlotte, brittleness giving

way to uncertainty in the face of Millie's continued hesitation. 'Please, Millie.' Before Charlotte's tears started in earnest. 'I need someone to tell me that I can do this and that everything's going to be okay.'

'Oh, Charlotte. Sweetie.' Millie was on her feet, wrapping her arms around Charlotte. Contact and comfort. Charlotte gulped back a sob. 'It *will* be okay. I know you. There's nothing you can't do when you put your mind to it. You'll make a wonderful mother. You'll see.'

'What am I going to tell Greyson?' whispered Charlotte.

But to that, Millie had no answer.

Derek arrived an hour and a half later, bearing Thai takeaway for three and a six-pack of beer. 'I don't do feel-good films and I don't do tears,' he said. 'I'm here strictly to get the low-down on the Greenstone Foundation proposal.'

'Of course you are,' murmured Millie soothingly. 'Shall we eat first?'

'We should definitely eat first,' said a freshly composed Charlotte.

Derek eyed the sweets laden kitchen counter sceptically. 'You're into the crisis food,' he declared. 'I've lived in enough foster homes to know crisis food when I see it and crisis phone calls when I get one.'

'This crisis doesn't involve you directly,' said Charlotte.

'Then why am I here?'

'We needed a test male,' said Millie. 'And by *we*, I mean Charlotte. Strictly speaking, this isn't my crisis either— lucky for you.'

'Millie's going to observe and take notes,' said Charlotte. 'Derek, would you like a cold glass for your beer?'

'Hospitable,' said Millie. 'Nice touch.'

Charlotte poured beer for Derek with a relatively steady

hand, wine for Millie, and sparkling mineral water for herself.

'The mineral water could raise questions,' said Millie. 'Maybe you should pour yourself a glass of wine as well, even if you don't touch it. Derek, what do you think?'

'Huh?' said Derek.

'My mistake,' said Millie. 'Proceed.'

Charlotte set three places at the kitchen counter for eating. She set serving spoons to Derek's Thai offerings. 'You think I need to be more formal?' asked Charlotte. 'Because I can always set the dining table?'

'No, this is good,' said Millie. 'He needs to feel comfortable and relaxed. Derek, do you feel comfortable and relaxed?'

'I might if I knew what was going *on*,' muttered Derek.

Millie nodded sagely. 'Proceed.'

'I'm going to ask him about his work,' said Charlotte. 'Derek, how's the work? Research coming together well?'

'Is this a job interview?' asked Derek, hoeing into the food. 'Because if this is about the sidekick position for the Greenstone Foundation, I want more prep time. Seriously, Charlotte. You could do worse than consider me for the job.'

'Interesting,' said Mille. 'The man has his own agenda.' She turned to Charlotte. 'Greyson may well have his own agenda too.'

'Who's Greyson?' asked Derek.

'Formerly Thaddeus,' said Charlotte. 'In other words Gil. Gil Tyler. Of long pig fame. Millie can fill you in on the details later. The important thing is for you to put yourself in the role of dedicated research scientist and world traveller. We didn't think it'd be too much of a stretch for you. As for the foundation position, if it goes ahead you'd damn well better apply seeing as I wrote it with you in mind.'

'Seriously?' said Derek.

'Seriously.'

Derek beamed.

'Excellent work with the compliments,' said Millie, and to Derek, 'How are you feeling? Are you feeling relaxed?'

'Well, I *was*,' murmured Derek.

'I think it's time,' said Mille.

'Are you sure?' Charlotte didn't feel at all sure. 'I mean, he's hardly touched his beer.'

'It's time,' said Millie. 'It's just a practice run. Master the fear.'

'Okay.' Charlotte took a huge breath and reached for Millie's wine, only Millie was faster, holding it up and out of the way before Charlotte could get to it. Derek had his beer halfway to his lips so no joy there either. 'Derek, I'm pregnant.'

Derek's beer went down wrong. Derek surfaced all a splutter.

'I'm thinking you should probably wait until Greyson's *between* beers to make that particular announcement,' said Millie.

'Will do,' said Charlotte nervously. 'Derek? Anything to add?'

'Not a word,' wheezed the beleaguered Derek.

'Put yourself in Greyson's shoes,' said Millie encouragingly. 'Anything to add *now*?'

'Am I the father?' asked Derek. 'No, let me rephrase. I can't say those particular words without breaking into a cold sweat. Is Greyson the father?'

'Yes,' said Charlotte.

'And also your fiancé.'

'No,' said Charlotte. 'I'm currently fiancé-less. As is Greyson.'

'And you want him back?' asked Derek.

'Hard to say,' murmured Charlotte. 'I never really had him in the first place. Let's just assume that I don't really know *what* I want from him at this particular point in time.'

'Do you want financial assistance when it comes to raising this child?' asked Derek.

'No.' Charlotte shook her head emphatically. 'I don't need Greyson's money. That's the last thing I need.' She picked up her glass of fizzy water, wishing it were wine. 'Is that really one of the first things that came to mind?'

'Yes,' said Derek grimly. 'Not everyone can afford to be blasé when it comes to ongoing monetary commitments, Charlotte, and raising a child very definitely qualifies as that.'

'So maybe she tells him she doesn't want his money *before* she tells him she's pregnant,' said Millie.

'How?' asked Charlotte. 'How do I do that?'

'Maybe you start with what you *do* want from him,' said Millie. 'Which would be…?' And when Charlotte remained silent, 'This is your cue. What do you want from him?'

But Charlotte didn't know. 'Maybe, apart from the knowing…maybe some level of participation?'

'You mean marriage,' said Derek.

'No! Not necessarily.' Charlotte was starting to tremble now. She countered by crossing her arms in front of her. 'I don't know. This isn't going well, is it?' she said in a small voice.

'You're telling a man he's going to be a father, Charlotte,' muttered Derek. 'How do you expect it to go?'

'Better,' she said and choked down her rising panic. 'I just assumed that breaking the news to him in person would be better, but maybe it's not. I could email him with the news, or text him, and *then* arrange a meeting...'

But Derek was shaking his head. 'I didn't say don't give him the news in person. I said give him some thinking time once you do. Don't analyse his initial response. Like as not, it won't be the one you want. Give him some space with this. Let him know *your* thoughts on marriage and motherhood, and then *let him be.*'

'I can do that,' said Charlotte faintly, and turned to Millie. Millie who'd been judging her presentation and hopefully taking notes. 'Millie, so how did it go?'

'Fine. Just fine,' said Millie a little too readily. And then, 'I need another drink.'

Charlotte waited until the following morning to email Greyson. A beautiful late-summer's morning with not a whisper of a cloud in the sky. A good day, she decided, for sharing unexpected news. Nonetheless, her email to Greyson still took her all morning to construct and finally consisted of three short words. 'Where are you?'

Greyson's reply pinged back within ten minutes. 'Hawkesbury river.'

'Dinner at my place this evening?' she wrote back, before she lost her nerve entirely. 'Seven p.m.?'

This time his reply came almost instantaneously. 'Why?'

Not a man bent on being amiable. Not entirely unexpected, given that her parting words to him two months ago had been, 'Don't call me and I won't call you.'

'Need to talk to you,' she wrote back. Now there was a phrase guaranteed to send a chill up a man's spine.

Charlotte sat back and stared at the computer screen after that, sat there for ten minutes with her heart in her throat, waiting for a reply that did not come. When the phone rang, she almost slipped her skin. Charlotte reached for it gingerly, hoping it was Greyson, hoping it was not.

'Charlotte Greenstone,' she said as evenly as she could, while her hands shook and her knees shook and she tucked her free hand between her knees in an effort to stop the trembling of both.

'So talk.' Greyson's voice; deep and gravelly and riddled with wariness.

'Hello, Greyson,' she said, in a voice that wobbled only faintly. 'I half expected you to be in Borneo.'

'No.'

'No.' She ran through the script she'd prepared in her mind. Some sort of compliment was supposed to come next, but her brain had gone blank the minute she'd heard that familiar deep voice.

'What do you want, Charlotte?'

'Not money.' She remembered Derek's words of last night and figured she might as well get that one out of the way. 'You don't ever need to worry on that score.'

'I wasn't,' he uttered dryly.

'Because money's not the problem here.'

'So what *is* the problem here?' he said. 'I'm assuming you're not ringing because life felt empty without me and you want to pick up where we left off? Am I wrong?'

Charlotte closed her eyes. She hadn't armoured herself properly against Greyson's thinly veiled hostility. She should have. 'Never mind,' she said raggedly. 'This was a really bad idea. I'm sorry. I shouldn't have bothered you.'

'Charlotte, wait!'

She waited in silence. Trembling. Quailing.

'Dinner, you said,' he muttered, and his voice was as ragged as hers.

'Yes.'

'You should know that I'll not be able to keep my hands off you if we have it at your place. You should know not to be with me in private right now. I'm telling you this as a courtesy.'

'Somewhere else, then,' she managed, while his words seared through her, bringing equal parts heat and apprehension. 'There are dozens of restaurants nearby.'

'Name one.'

She did. A steakhouse slash cocktail bar. Nothing fancy but there was privacy to be had in darkened booths if conversation demanded it, and this conversation surely would.

'I'll meet you there at seven,' he said. 'And, Charlotte?'

'What?' she said faintly.

'If you want me to be at all civilised, you'll be letting me pay for the meal.'

Greyson Tyler was no stranger to trouble. He knew the ways in which it crept up on a man. He knew how it smelled. He knew without a shadow of a doubt that meeting Charlotte again for a meal and whatever else she had in mind spelled trouble for them both. His needs were a little too intense when it came to delectable yet thoroughly unsuitable Charlotte Greenstone. There was no telling what he might demand of her, or the concessions he might make in order to get those demands met.

He'd stayed away. He'd been the gentleman and kept his distance. He'd done everything she'd asked of him and, *dammit*, he'd been hurt in the process.

Cancel.

That was what he *should* do. Tell her she'd been right all along about them wanting different types of lives, and that he couldn't see any reason to meet up with her again. No reason at all.

Cancel.

But he did not.

Greyson arrived fifteen minutes early to the restaurant Charlotte had suggested: a scarred and bluesy corner bar with a blackboard menu promising quality fare that didn't cost the earth. A quick glance around told him that Charlotte hadn't yet arrived. He ordered a beer, found a shadowy corner booth with a view of the entrance and settled down to wait.

Charlotte the wilful, the reckless, the vulnerable. Best lover he'd ever had. Unstinting in her responses and mesmerising in her sexual abandon. Not a woman any man would forget in a hurry and he cursed her afresh while he sat with his beer and waited, and nursed the scars she'd given him.

He didn't know why he was here—lining up for another serve of nameless sorrow—except that she'd asked him to meet her and she'd sounded so unsure of herself and that in itself signalled trouble. Maybe her workmates had found out about her fictional fiancé. Maybe she'd lost her job and her reputation—*her* problem, not his—but he would hear her out and help if he could. He could do that much without letting bitterness hold sway.

They'd only been on a handful of dates. Hardly her fault if her withdrawal had come too late to save him from going under. He could give her that much.

Honour demanded it.

Grey saw Charlotte before she spotted him. Small

woman with generous curves and a waterfall of wavy black hair pulled back off her face with a vibrant silk headband. She wore tailored black trousers, dainty high-heeled sandals, and a sleeveless vest top in the same pinks, purples, and greens as her headband. A purple leather handbag completed the outfit, and she looked more like the pampered socialite he'd taken to his mother's barbecue than the experienced Associate Professor of Archaeology he knew her to be.

He stood as she approached him. Stood because a woman who expected a man to open car doors for her would surely expect that as well. Stood because the fighter in him demanded he pursue any advantage he could with her and size was one of them.

She cast him a quick smile and slid into the bench seat opposite. A waiter materialised and took her order for mineral water. Greyson's beer stood mostly untouched and he left it that way.

'Thank you for coming,' she said politely.

'I'm a sucker for punishment.' Nothing but the truth. 'I'm also curious as to what you have to say to me.'

'Ah,' said Charlotte. 'Yes. That. I kind of need to work my way up to that particular discussion. How's your mother?'

'My mother's well.' Not where he'd been expecting this conversation to go. 'Why?'

'No reason. How's the Sarah situation?'

'I've seen her once since we spoke after the barbecue. We talked. She left. She blames you, by the way, for my newfound insensitivity.'

'Handy,' she said quietly.

Charlotte's drink came and the waiter directed them to the blackboard menu. Neither he nor Charlotte was ready to order. 'You've lost weight,' he said. She still took his breath away with her perfection of form and features, but there was no denying she'd dropped a few kilos from her slender frame. Kilos she could ill afford to lose.

She'd lost weight; she looked wan. He was the son of a doctor. 'Charlotte, are you sick?'

Grey watched in horror as tears swam in Charlotte's eyes and threatened to overflow.

Oh, God, she *was* sick. 'What is it?' Information. He needed information.

'Not sick,' she murmured. 'Not sick.' She put her hand to her forehead for a moment, then changed her mind and put both hands in her lap. Not once did she meet his gaze. She stared at her coaster, the tabletop, the entrance to the bar as if she'd rather be anywhere else but there with him. 'Pregnant.'

'*What?*'

Charlotte glanced up at him then, startled and terrified and apologetic all at once and he had his answer.

'Mine,' he said.

'Yes.' He could hardly hear her for the thundering of his heart. 'There's tests we can do if that's what you want,' she offered. 'But there's been no one else.'

'Forget the tests.' Satisfaction flooded through him, as unexpected as it was savage.

Mine.

In which case… 'Shouldn't you be putting *on* weight?' he said silkily.

'I'm working on it,' she said in a low raw voice. 'I've also been thinking about what we might do. Greyson, I don't want to raise this child all by myself. It's not enough. *I'm* not enough. A child should have more than that. More family. More security.'

'You want a termination?' Hard to keep his jaw from clenching or his dislike of that notion from colouring his words. 'Is that what you brought me here to tell me? Because it's not going to enamour you to me, Charlotte. Not by a long shot.'

Mine.

'That's not why I asked you here,' she murmured. 'I've not considered that course of action. I don't think it's for me.'

'Good.'

The waiter approached them again, took one look at Grey and kept right on walking.

'I'm not asking for marriage or monetary support either,' she said earnestly.

'Tough.' From one have-it-my-way child to another. 'You're getting both. And food. We're ordering food *now*. Pick something.'

'I'll have the chef's salad.'

'Now pick something *else*.'

'And the teriyaki chicken kebabs,' she said with a roll of her eyes. 'But only because I'm humouring you.'

Grey glared at her. Better that than leaning across the table and kissing her senseless. Or was it?

In the end he did lean across and kiss her, terrified that she wouldn't respond to him, equally terrified when she did because it was still there, this all-consuming need to lose himself in her. 'Pick a date,' he murmured when his lips left hers. 'Any date.'

'I'm not marrying you, Greyson. There's no need for that. Not in this day and age.'

'If you really think I'm going to let my child be raised a bastard, you really don't know me very well,' he said grimly.

'My point exactly,' countered Charlotte. 'Greyson, we hardly know one another. What I do know of you suggests that marriage is the last thing on your mind, and that you'd start to feel trapped within five minutes of taking that step. You've already broken one engagement because you weren't prepared to settle for a life based in Sydney.'

Grey stared at Charlotte broodingly. He couldn't deny it. He liked his freedom, and he loved to travel, but, dammit, was it so wrong to want this child to be born within marriage?'

'The baby could still have your name,' said Charlotte. 'Access wouldn't be a problem. I *want* you in this baby's life. But we don't have to get married for that to happen.'

'You think I'll take it, don't you?' he said bleakly. 'The easy way out. The half measure. You think I'll be content to stand at the periphery of this child's life, never quite giving or getting enough.'

'Greyson, I—'

'You're wrong.'

'Lofty words for a man who intends to spend the next three years of his life in Borneo.'

'I didn't take that job,' he said tightly. 'Something you would have discovered weeks ago had you thought enough of me to stick around.'

'I thought enough of you to bring you back, didn't I?' She looked mutinous, and scared, and sorry, and she made his heart bleed.

'No. You're scared enough of your inadequacies as a single parent to bring me back. You're looking for a back-up plan for this child in case something happens to you, and, unfortunately, I'm all you've got.'

If Charlotte had looked wan before, she now looked positively waxy. 'This is never going to work,' she said faintly.

'Are you going to faint?' Dear heaven, she looked fragile, and anxious, and perilously close to tears. 'Don't you dare faint!'

'I'm not going to faint.'

'Or cry.'

'Or cry,' she said in a voice that threatened exactly that.

Greyson eyed her grimly. 'You should know something about me, Charlotte. I never give up. I make things work. It's what I do.' He cupped her neck in his hand and touched his lips to hers again, hard and fast and ruthless. 'I'm free next Tuesday. What say we get married then?'

CHAPTER EIGHT

DINNER wasn't going well. Charlotte hadn't anticipated that Greyson would see straight through to her fear of leaving this child all alone in the world should something happen to her. She hadn't planned on his kisses reducing her to jelly and she certainly hadn't anticipated that his heated insistence on marriage would wash over her like a panacea, or that the thought of marriage to this man would be so very tempting.

'Greyson, I thank you for the offer,' she said raggedly. 'Truly, I do, but *think*. You're talking about a marriage of necessity, not a union based on love. Is that really what you want?'

Greyson remained silent. Such a beautiful man, so hell-bent on doing the right thing by her and this baby, that he couldn't see through to what he might need, and what he would lose if he insisted on a marriage of convenience.

'What about your work?' she continued. 'If not Borneo this time, you'll want to go somewhere else down the track. Greyson, you know my feelings on that kind of life.'

'We'll compromise,' he said, in a voice that promised anything but. 'I don't have all the answers for you, Charlotte. I have three more months' work here. After that I had planned on taking on a new project but it doesn't have to be out of the country. Maybe it's time I looked to my own backyard and reassessed my future direction. Maybe it's time you did the same.'

'I want to finish up at the university and set up a Greenstone Archaeology Foundation,' she offered. 'One that finances and manages archaeological projects and gets key people working together. I'd start small. One project at a time. If I can get the right people in place, I'll be able to work part time from home.'

'Or anywhere else,' he said silkily.

'Is that your idea of compromise? We traipse the world with you?'

'Of what use is a father to a child if he's never *there*? Jesus, Charlotte. What is it you *want* from me?' Greyson glared at her, a man trapped.

Trapped because of her.

'Not marriage,' she said, and her heart bled for herself and for Greyson, and the baby they'd unwittingly made. 'Not without love. Something else. Something that love doesn't necessarily have to play a part in. I'm arranging for my own work to become more flexible so that I can be a hands-on mother. You've no idea how relieved I am that you want to be a hands-on father. I'm just saying that there's no need to rush into marriage. Truly. We have the time and the resources to come up with a solution that doesn't necessarily involve for ever and ever, amen.'

Greyson closed his eyes, shook his head. Probably wishing himself halfway up the Sepik River. Anywhere but here.

'My work's probably going to get a little chaotic over the next few months while I set up a foundation blueprint,' she began, and Greyson's eyes snapped open.

'As long as it's not a dangerously exhausting plan, I'm all for it,' he said smoothly. 'Could you base your foundation headquarters at the Double Bay house?'

'Yes.' This was where she wanted this conversation to go. Exactly where she wanted it to go. 'It's the logical choice, especially if the baby and I lived there too.' Tell him what you want, Derek had told her. Not marriage, not without love, but something that might suit them both and allow them to raise a child and still partake of the work they loved. 'I don't know that you've been around the back of Aurora's place but the grounds flow all the way down to the harbour. There's a boat house down there— big enough for a speedboat, nothing more. There's a jetty and a deepwater mooring there too.'

Charlotte thought she saw a flicker of interest in Greyson's dark eyes but if he had any thoughts on how that deepwater mooring might best be put to use, he kept them to himself.

'You'd be welcome there. Living in the house or on your boat. You might not always be there, what with your work and your travels, but you could base there. We could all base there. That's kind of as far as I've gone with the thinking.'

'It's sound thinking,' he murmured. 'God, Charlotte. You're going to have to give me some time with this.'

'Of course.' Charlotte picked up her mineral water and sipped it through the straw. She looked to the bar. She looked at the artwork on the walls. She'd known this meeting would be a hard one. But she'd seriously underestimated just how hard it would be, or how bad she would feel about being the tool of Greyson's entrapment. 'Greyson—I'm so sorry.'

'Don't,' he said gruffly. 'Please, Charlotte. Just… I need some time to think.'

She gave him time. Seconds that felt like hours. Minutes that stretched into eternity. Much more of this and she was going to start rocking back and forward keening, such was her nervous tension.

'All right,' he said finally. 'I accept your offer to base myself and my operations at the Double Bay house with you, under one condition.'

'What's the condition?'

'Marry me. Tie up your money and your possessions so I can't get to them if that's what you're worried about, but marry me.'

'No.' He wasn't the only one around here with a stubborn streak the size of the pyramids. 'Not without love.'

'What makes you think you won't get that too?' Greyson at his most formidable, but the chill in his eyes was at odds with his words and a perfect example of what she *didn't* want their relationship to be.

'You won't love me if I trap you into a life you loathe, Greyson. You'll hate me.'

He was back to scowling at her. Back to brooding.

'Three months,' she bargained desperately. 'Give us three months, and during that time we live together in the house on the hill and we sort out our work and we try and make space in our lives for this baby and for each other. Surely you can see the sense in that?'

But he shook his head. 'Half measures don't suit me, Charlotte. They never have, and truth be told I don't see much sense in postponing our marriage at all. But...' his beautiful mouth twisted into a mockery of a smile '...in the spirit of compromise, I'll give you these next three months free of matrimony. With one caveat.'

'Which is?' she asked warily.

'That if we live together, we give it our best shot. No holding back. No behaving like polite strangers. And no separate bedrooms.'

'That's three caveats.'

'No, it's not.' His knuckles were white as he reached for his beer. Charlotte wasn't the only one around here so tense she could snap. 'It's just three different ways of saying the same thing.'

Charlotte's food intake was abysmal but Grey coaxed and connived and eventually she cleared her plate. He put his mind to amiable conversation. He stayed away from topics like parenthood and work commitments because, frankly, he was still processing their earlier conversation about those. He paid for their meal and insisted on walking Charlotte home. He bought her a gelato along the way and Charlotte rolled her eyes and protested that she was too full for ice cream, but she ate nearly half of it and Grey finished off the rest.

He took a fair stab at pretending that the world beneath his feet hadn't just irrevocably shifted out of his reach.

He kept his hands to himself until he got to Charlotte's apartment door, and when she unlocked it, and asked where he was parked and whether he wanted to come in, he shoved his hands in his pockets and leaned against the wall. He'd bargained hard for this very concession: no holding back, no distance between them. He hadn't bargained on being afraid to take advantage of it.

'When do you want me to move into the house?' he asked gruffly. 'I figure I can get the cat there in a couple of days, weather willing.'

'I can be there from tomorrow onwards.' She looked so beautiful standing there in the doorway to her apartment. Hard to believe that such a small frame could contain a will that more than matched his own. 'I'll get removalists in at the weekend to pack up and shift all this stuff across.'

'You won't keep your apartment as a bolt hole?'

'No. You wanted all in, remember? If I keep this place I *would* be tempted to retreat here when the going got tough.'

Charlotte looked nervous. He far preferred her not. 'Pessimist,' he murmured. 'It might not even *get* tough.'

She sent him a disbelieving glance. He countered with a slow smile. 'There are benefits to having a man around the house that you haven't even dreamed of yet,' he said.

'Oh, really?'

'Oh, yes.'

'We'll see.' She leaned against the door, more relaxed than he'd seen her all evening. 'Do you cook?'

'Not often, but I hunt and I can gather.'

'Do you clean?'

'No, but I do appreciate a tidy house.'

'Do you iron?'

'That's what laundry services are for.'

'Do you mow?' she asked silkily.

'What? And do a groundsman out of his job?'

'Greyson, you've spent the last dozen or so years living out of a suitcase, eating hotel food and answering to no one. You're not even housebroken. I'd go easy on the promises of domestic bliss if I were you.'

'If you say so, dear,' he murmured. 'Little phrase I picked up from my father. Like it?'

'Yes, but it's a little early in the relationship for weary resignation, don't you think? You need to keep that in reserve.'

'Noted.'

'Are you coming in?' she asked again, so Greyson stepped inside and she closed the door behind him, and he stood there.

All in.

Same priceless painting on the wall. Same wickedly expensive furnishings.

Totally different situation.

'Coffee?' she offered.

'No.'

'Cognac? Liqueur? Scotch?'

He remembered the Scotch from last time, and the raw and desperate lovemaking that had followed. 'Absolutely not!' He needed no encouragement in the raw and desperate department. He was there already. 'And none for you either.'

Charlotte's sandals came off. Her eyes had narrowed. 'Someone's having a panic attack around here,' she murmured. 'And it's not me.'

'I'm not panicking.' It was more of a cold sweat and it had nothing to do with the enormity of the changes he was about to make to his life. No, he was far too busy sweating the small stuff. Like that for all his expertise in the area of biological interactions, he didn't know the first thing about making love to a pregnant woman.

'Are you going to sit down?' she murmured.

'Probably not.' Not the lounge. Probably best to avoid the lounge. God, his nerves were shot. He crossed to the window and stared out at the view.

Charlotte crossed to the sidebar and poured a hefty belt of Scotch into a glass and brought it over to him, and placed it in his hand. 'Drink,' she said gently. 'You don't want to ruin all your fine and heroic rhetoric by going into shock.'

Greyson grimaced, but he put the glass to his lips and drank it down in one long swallow.

'Oh, the *envy*,' she murmured, and he smiled a little at that but his eyes remained guarded. A woman looking for joy in their depths would be disappointed. A woman looking to Greyson to hold her and make everything feel all right—if only for a little while—was disappointed too.

'Are you scared?' he asked gruffly.

Such a simple question from a deeply complex man.

'Terrified,' she whispered, and exposed her soul and all its flaws completely. 'Absolutely terrified.'

And then his arms came around her, strong and infinitely gentle. His lips were gentle too, and his taste was one she'd tried hard to forget. 'It's okay,' he murmured, as he slid his hands through her hair and cradled her head to his chest. 'It's going to be okay. I promise.'

Charlotte wanted to believe him. She wanted to believe that her baby would have a father to look to, and that she wasn't alone in this. She wanted badly to believe that Greyson was here for her now and here he would stay. That he would domesticate easily and be content. That she would find the home and the family she'd been searching for all her life.

She desperately wanted to believe all those things.

But she could not.

Two days later, Greyson moored his cat at Charlotte's jetty in Sydney Harbour. His view of the Bridge, Circular Quay, and the Opera House was one to make angels weep. The turmoil Charlotte's steadfast refusal to marry him had instilled in him would have made Satan crow.

Grey *knew* the value of family. Of marriage, solid and binding. Hell, Charlotte only had to look to herself to see how insecure not being part of a family unit made a child feel. So why wouldn't she just do the right thing and *marry* him?

So what if he hadn't lived a regular life for a while? He'd grown up in a house, gone to school in the suburbs, he knew how it worked. He knew how to mow lawns and unpack groceries and take out the garbage. He knew how to peg out washing and clean a bathroom—his mother had seen to that, bless her iron-willed soul.

He could do this.

And then there were the things Grey didn't know how to do, he admitted reluctantly.

Like how to convince a stubborn woman that marriage was the only option for him and that love would come easier to *both* of them once a commitment had been made.

And how to make love to a woman with his baby in her belly, which was something he hadn't done yet but would, soon, just as soon as he got over his fear of doing something wrong.

By bedtime that night, Greyson was a mess and Charlotte was no better. They sat in the informal living room, watching the late-night weather together in silence. Charlotte, sitting on the couch with her legs tucked up beneath her, Greyson commanding one of the man-sized single chairs. Greyson cloaked his nervousness in stillness. Charlotte tried to do the same but her eyes followed his every movement, watchful and wary, and she jumped at every unexpected sound. Damn near drove him nuts with her quick smile and panicked eyes. Terrified—just like him—of what they'd begun.

'I might have to bed down on the catamaran tonight,' he said after the weather report had finished and he'd got to his feet. 'I really should make sure of the mooring this first night. Wouldn't want her to drift away on the tide.'

'No. No, of course not,' said Charlotte quickly, and stood as well. 'That would be bad.'

Charlotte nodded. Greyson nodded too. A festival of nodding, followed by a long and excrutiating silence.

'Can I get you any bedding?' Charlotte's words came out rushed and nervous. 'Blankets. Pillows. Stuff like that?'

'No. No, I have everything I need.'

'Of course.'

More silence. Pregnant woman nodding.

'So…goodnight?' said Charlotte finally. Did she look relieved that they wouldn't be sharing a bed? Hard to tell beneath the panic.

'Yeah, I'll see you in the morning. I'll come up before you go to work. We can do newspapers. Or breakfast. Something.'

'Sounds good,' said Charlotte. 'So…goodnight?'

'Night,' he muttered, and cursed himself for his fears and his awkwardness as he turned on his heel and fled.

Maybe Charlotte was right. Maybe these new living arrangements *would* take some getting used to. Maybe Charlotte's notion of easing their way into each other's lives hadn't been such a bad idea after all.

On day two of Greyson's incarceration at the mansion, he banished the crow on his shoulder to the farthest tree and started taking stock of the house and where he might fit in it. He needed an office, spacious and light filled, and he didn't think the second-floor sewing room would mind. The day came and went as treasures were found and ruthlessly vacuum sealed and boxed for storage. Greyson worked solidly and made hardly a dint when it came to the contents of that room. He was sorting and bagging yet another monstrous pile of brightly coloured cottons when Charlotte walked into the room, looking tired and not altogether pleased to see him. Or maybe it was just the chaos he'd created that offended her.

'Busy day?' she said from the doorway.

'No.'

'Don't you have papers to write?' she asked next.

'Yes.'

'But you've decided to take up patchwork quilting instead?'

'No, I'm stealing office space and banishing your godmother from the premises. I'm sure she was a wonderful woman, not to mention all the way eccentric and richer than Croesus, but I can't live with her. And while we're on topic, I'm not sure I can live with being a kept man, either. Somewhere along the line I expect to contribute towards this household's upkeep. I don't know how but it's something we need to talk about.'

Charlotte leaned against the doorway, and crossed her arms in front of her, all neat and tidy, as if she'd stepped straight out of *Businesswoman's Vogue*. It didn't escape Grey's notice that she looked completely at home in the luxurious surroundings. He really didn't know if such surrounds were ever going to suit him.

'You know, somewhere among all those dreamed-of benefits of having a man about the house was a dream where he greeted me cordially when I came home from work, asked me how my day had gone, *listened* when I told him, and maybe even poured me an icy cold hand-squeezed apple juice and soda with a dash of lime,' said Charlotte sweetly.

'What was he wearing?' asked Greyson.

'Not a lot.'

Grey peeled off his T-shirt and dropped it to the sofa, perfectly willing to oblige. 'That better?'

'Well, it's a start.'

Grey looked around at the chaos he'd created with his emptying of cupboards and drawers. All that storage space, and every inch of it crammed full. 'It's a work in progress.

And I'm guessing you probably had a bad day at the office. You've got that look.'

'I either got fired or I resigned,' she said reluctantly. 'Depends who you ask.'

'You don't need them anyway.' Grey abandoned the cottons in favour of closing the gap between them. 'And I guarantee they're going to regret losing you.'

'I'm beginning to appreciate your appeal,' she said with a smile that was way too small for her.

'Wait till you try my hand-squeezed apple juice with soda and lime.' He drew closer, and, gathering courage, traced his fingers down her arm until he reached her hand. Such a fine and delicate hand, and he was careful as he threaded his fingers through hers, stepped past her and tugged her gently towards the hallway. Touching Charlotte settled him in a way that he hadn't been settled all day.

'Where are we going?' asked Charlotte, but she followed willingly in his wake, and her fingers had curled around his, and that was something.

'Kitchen to get you a drink and something to eat.'

'You mean milk and cookies?'

'Do we have milk and cookies?' he asked, glancing back at her. He'd rummaged around in the commercial-sized kitchen at lunchtime. The cupboards had been mostly bare.

'No,' she said with the hint of a smile.

Something to do tomorrow, then. Shop.

'You were right about Aurora,' said Charlotte when they were halfway down the first-floor stairs. 'She could be a little eccentric. She never actually *did* any patchwork quilting that I recall. She just liked buying the materials. And I really don't know what to do with a lot of her collections. I was thinking of donating them to a university or a museum, although clearly not the university I no longer work for. Colour me a woman scorned.'

'Make them the property of the Greenstone Foundation, get a curator in to put together a touring collection, and send it around the galleries,' Grey offered by way of a solution. 'It'll promote your foundation, preserve Aurora's name, and get it out of your hair.'

'*Your* hair,' she said.

'That too.'

They'd reached the kitchen. Grey sat her on a stool and, reluctantly forgoing the touch of her hand, he set about fixing her a soda and lime, no apples. He served it with an unrepentant smile. 'You have to imagine the apples. I'm assuming this won't be too hard for you, given what you're *capable* of imagining.'

'Gil would have flung himself into the harbour and swum its length to get me apples for this juice,' Charlotte told him loftily.

'Yes, but then he'd have been hit by a paddle steamer on his way back and sliced up into apple-flavoured fish bait,' countered Grey. 'Gil had no sense of his own mortality.'

Charlotte allowed her smile to widen.

'So how much notice do you have to give the university that you're finishing up?' he asked, getting back to the issue at hand.

'Two weeks, one of which can be taken as leave. I'm tempted to take two of my colleagues with me. Millie, who you've met. And Derek, who you haven't met yet. I've a mind to make Derek the foundation's second in command and put him in charge of the digs. Derek's useful and he knows how to lead. He thought Gil was an idiot too.'

'Did he now?' said Grey darkly. 'Maybe we'll bond.'

'Of course, chances are Derek still thinks *you're* Gil,' murmured Charlotte. 'Unless Millie's told him otherwise.

Millie knows you're you. You being the stranger whose office she procured. I'm pretty sure she'd have mentioned you to Derek by now. Derek and Millie being an item. I'm assuming they talk between themselves.'

'Never assume,' said Grey. 'You wouldn't rather employ two people who *weren't* an item?'

'Don't know,' said Charlotte. 'Acquiring and managing employees will be a new experience for me. Any thoughts you have on that will be most appreciated. The plan is to catch on fast.'

'And not wear yourself out.'

'And work from home,' said Charlotte. 'This home. Which is why I'm thinking we should do a walk through now and make sure we're thinking similarly when it comes to which rooms to allocate to what.'

'Eyes off my sewing room,' said Grey.

'Keep your sewing room,' countered Charlotte. 'But I *am* thinking of turning over the ground-floor eastern wing of the house to foundation business. What do you think?'

'Tell me what you want shifted and I'll shift it,' said Grey.

'You *are* useful.'

'Never doubt it.'

They walked through the house, making plans and talking big until at last they reached the part of the house where all the bedrooms were and there they fell silent.

'You said you wanted to share a bedroom,' murmured Charlotte. 'And a bed.'

'Yep.' Grey shoved his hands in his pockets and stared into a massive bedroom with more floor space than the average house. The bed looked huge too, but there was only one of them, which was also what he'd intended, but the more he looked at it, the greater his apprehension about making love to a pregnant Charlotte grew. 'That's what I said.'

'Any further reflections on that?'

'Plenty.'

'Anything we need to discuss?'

'Probably.'

'You slept on the boat last night,' she said tentatively. 'Was it because you didn't want to sleep with me?'

'Charlotte—' How to explain his hesitation without sounding like an idiot? 'It's not you. It's just—' Apparently there was *no* way of saying this without sounding like an idiot. 'I've never made love to a pregnant woman before,' he admitted gruffly. 'I'm not a small man. You're pregnant. Fragile. What if I hurt you? What if I hurt the baby?'

'Is *that* what you're worried about?' Charlotte looked amused. Relieved.

'It's not all I'm worried about, no, but at the moment that's what tops the list. And don't look at me like that. It's a valid concern.'

Charlotte smiled. Charlotte walked his way until she stood directly in front of him. She took his hand and placed it on her still-flat belly, her hand atop his. Greyson's heart hammered once and settled to an unsteady rhythm. Impending fatherhood was going to take some getting used to.

'Our baby is well protected,' she murmured. 'Our baby's *mother* has no intention of spending another night like the last one. Worrying like crazy about all the things she's taken away from you, and wishing you were there beside her so she could at least give something back. Our baby's mother has no intention of denying herself the pleasure of your embrace. In point of fact, she's thinking she should probably address those concerns of yours right now.'

'How?'

'Directly.' Her hand atop his as she encouraged him to slide it higher, past her waist and on to the generous curve of her breast. 'She wants you to stop worrying about nothing. She needs to know she still pleases you in this regard.'

'Charlotte—'

'Greyson.'

One name a plea for mercy. The other full of rich amusement and gentle reassurance.

The future mother of Grey's child unbuttoned her blouse with her free hand. Slid it aside to reveal a lacy lavender half-cup bra. Beneath it lay flesh, warm and beckoning. Grey stroked the edge where lace met skin with his fingertips. He leaned forward and gently pressed a kiss to Charlotte's lips.

Charlotte responded as she'd always responded. Generously. Wantonly. Threatening his control and bringing him to instant aching arousal. Her next kiss slid deeper and promised all that he wanted and more.

'I should have known something was amiss when even the scrape of a bath towel made my breasts tighten and ache for your mouth on them,' she whispered. 'I thought I was just remembering you. Reliving the things you did to me and the things I did to you. Do you remember the things I did to you, Greyson?'

'Charlotte, have mercy,' he muttered, even as he slid her shirt from her shoulders. Her hair came down next and he slid his fingers through the tresses, glorying in its abundance and the silky-soft feel of it. Slow down, he wanted to say. Slow down so that I can too. So I can do this right and stay in control. But he didn't say any of that, just cupped her face in his hands and kissed her again and when she wound her arms around his neck, and when her eyes were suitably passion-glazed, he lifted her up and carried her to the bed.

'You'll have to stop that,' she murmured as he laid her gently on the bed and eased down beside her, careful where he put his weight, careful of everything.

'Stop what?'

'Thinking. Measuring. Assessing. I don't want careful from you, Greyson. Not in this.'

'Then what do you want?' he said as he lowered his head to her breast and pressed an open-mouth kiss to the curve of it. He tugged her bra aside and found her nipple next and this time the homage he paid her was a little more urgent. Charlotte strained against him, urging him to more so he gave her more and she whimpered her approval. 'Tell me what you want.'

'Everything.'

Sleeping arrangements sorted to mutual and blissful satisfaction, Charlotte turned her mind to turning part of Aurora's Double Bay home into Greenstone Foundation HQ. Millie accepted the admin position Charlotte offered her. Derek accepted the Project Manager's position. Generous wages plus voting positions for them both on the foundation's board of directors. The latter being Greyson's suggestion; his thoughts being that if she had to have a board of directors, better to have at least some people on it who were responsible for the work and who could speak for it.

Charlotte thought it a good idea. Greyson had a great many good ideas when it came to the running of the foundation. He could be very supportive, could Greyson.

And then, with his next breath he could hit her with a question she had no idea how to answer. Like, 'When do you want to tell my family that you're pregnant?' They were still in discussion over that one.

'Not yet,' she said, dreading the thought of sharing her baby news with Greyson's family and watching Olivia's eyes ice over.

'When?'

'After the first trimester. Wouldn't want them getting all joyous and then not have this baby come to pass.'

Grey looked at her with those eyes that sometimes saw clear through to her soul, ignoring her not-so-honest pre- diction of a joyful response and cutting straight to the heart of her fears.

'You think they won't be pleased.'

'I think they have a right to their opinions,' said Charlotte carefully. 'I think—under the circumstances— that they could probably be forgiven for wishing that you'd never set eyes on me.'

'They'll come round,' said Greyson firmly. 'Charlotte, give them a chance.'

'I will. And I know we have to tell them, and we will tell them. Soon. Just not yet.'

'Then how about we invite my mother to join us for lunch this week? Not here. Somewhere neutral. Just my mother. No baby talk. Just a straight letting her get to know you.'

He hadn't forgotten their conversation about how to in- troduce a woman to his family, bless him. But the thought of meeting Olivia again, and doing her best to impress, and potentially having Olivia remain singularly unimpressed, gave Charlotte pause.

'Where does she think you're living these days?' asked Charlotte, and this time it was Greyson's turn to look dis- comfited. 'She still thinks you're living on the cat, here in the harbour somewhere, doesn't she?'

'Probably.' Greyson eyed her steadily. 'I've no objection to telling her that we're living together. I can do it today.'

'Okay,' said Charlotte faintly. 'Maybe we should start with that.'

'And the invitation for her to join us for lunch?'

'Is a good idea.' The man was just full of good ideas. 'I know that. Olive branch and all that. Fresh start. No Sarah there to give your mother conflicting loyalties. Does your mother still see Sarah on occasion, do you think?'

'I believe they get together for coffee every now and again.'

Great. Just great.

'Charlotte, Sarah's out of the picture.'

'Because of the baby,' said Charlotte, feeling very, very small.

'Because of many things,' said Greyson gently. 'None of which are related to you.'

'She's still going to think I've trapped you when she finds out about the baby.'

'Charlotte, I'm not *trapped.*'

Yes, he was. He just didn't know it yet. Trapped into fatherhood, but at least she'd spared him from being bound to her by marriage. That much, she could give him and *would* give him if he didn't come to love her the way she was fast learning to love him. 'You're a rare and beautiful man, Greyson Tyler. I couldn't have wished for a better father for this child.'

'Marry me,' he said instantly.

'No.'

'Why not?'

'Because I'm not ready to take that step yet,' she said gently. 'And neither are you. First things first.'

Frustration rolled off Greyson in waves. Impatience.

Action man wanted action. He thrived on it and always would. Just one more very good reason for him to be perfectly sure of his feelings before buying into Charlotte's sedentary and peaceful life.

'All right. First things first,' Greyson said curtly. Not their first difference of opinion and it wouldn't be their last. 'Let's just meet my mother for lunch. See how it goes.'

'Okay,' Charlotte agreed, and fought to quell her instant and overwhelming apprehension. All her life she'd dreamed of having a family and this was her chance to secure Greyson's. Her child would have grandparents. Grandparents who loved and adored their grandchild, and that could happen, and probably *would* happen, provided Olivia's resistance towards Charlotte didn't get in the way.

'Okay,' she said again. 'Let's arrange to have lunch with your mother. I'm all for it. I am. But maybe next week rather than this week. This week's full.'

He gave her thirty days of household bliss. Thirty days and thirty nights of unstinting support and manly perfection, with nary a mother in sight, and on the thirty-first day a job offer came in for him and turned Charlotte's world upside down.

'I want you to read something,' he said on Charlotte's return from yet another meeting with her solicitors about the set-up of a Greenstone Foundation board of directors. He'd placed his laptop on the kitchen counter and opened up an email addressed to him. The email was titled Galapagos Project Leader Position and a little red exclamation mark next to it signalled the need for a prompt response.

'Who's Eleanor Stratten?' she asked, for that was who the email was from.

'She's a department head at CSIRO. Plant physiology. Bigwig. Very big wig.'

Charlotte scanned the first paragraph. Once-in-a-lifetime research opportunity, fully funded two-year project based around the Galapagos Islands. Project head needed, Eleanor had heard on the grapevine that Greyson was available. Details attached, was he interested?

Charlotte straightened. Greyson handed her a long tall glass of freshly squeezed apple juice and ginger beer with a twist of lime and a spoonful of mint. 'You haven't opened the attachment,' he murmured.

'I don't need to.'

'It's not based in the Galapagos,' he said. 'It can be run from here.'

Charlotte nodded and sipped her drink for good measure.

'There'd be travel, of course,' he said, not taking her entirely for a fool. 'A lot of back and forth. I'm not saying I wouldn't be away for weeks at a time, maybe longer.'

'You should do it,' she said. 'It's a once-in-a-lifetime opportunity.' Charlotte wanted to sound sincere but her voice came out all brittle and wrong. She'd known from the start that she'd never keep him anchored here, not without destroying everything he was and denying him all that he could be. 'When does it start?'

'Almost immediately. The team is already assembled and ready to go. They had a project leader sorted too. His wife had a stroke.'

'I'm sorry to hear that.' Charlotte set her drink on the counter and summoned up a smile. 'It really does sound like a wonderful opportunity for you.'

'Charlotte, it's the *Galapagos*.'

'I know.' No other place on earth could match it when it came to finding evidence for the evolution of the species. This job offer was the equivalent of someone walking up to an archaeologist and asking them if they wanted to be part of an expedition to the lost city of Atlantis. 'Holy Grail.'

'I'd still be based here. I'd do everything I could to ensure that I'd be here for you when the baby comes. I'd not miss that. I'd make it a contract condition.'

Charlotte looked away. It shamed her that her first response had not been happiness for Greyson but dismay for herself. It terrified her to reflect on just how much she'd come to rely on his company and his support.

'Charlotte, please. I can't do what I've been doing this past month on a permanent basis. I've enjoyed every minute of it and I'll do it again willingly, but not all the time,' he said. 'My work is part of who I am. I can't not do it.'

'I know,' she said softly. 'I think this position is perfect for you. You'd be mad not to apply for it, and I don't want you mad. I don't want you frustrated or feeling like you're just marking time here either. I'll be fine. I have everything I could possibly need right here, and as you say…you'll be back and forward. I'll probably hardly even notice you're gone.'

'This *will* work out for us. We'll *make* it work,' Greyson said huskily, as if by saying the words he could make them come true.

'Confident man.'

'No,' he said. 'Not confident, not always. Just determined.'

Grey got the job. He'd known when Ellie had emailed him that his chances were good. He'd tailored his entire

working life towards this sort of project, building the skill
set he needed to land just such a gem. Always taking the
road less travelled. Never shying away from the difficult
turns. He didn't shy away from them now.

All in.

It was the way he'd always lived his life and it remained
to be seen if he could turn 'all in' into 'all in until Charlotte
needed him', at which point he'd have to be all out and
focusing on his life with her for a while. He'd need a good
second in command. He'd already been in touch with Joey
Tank, whose wife had had the stroke. She was home now
and improving daily. Joey had high hopes that she'd be as
good as new within a few months, or, more realistically,
within half a dozen months. Joey had taken long service
leave to be with his wife and he'd jumped at Grey's offer
to keep him in the project loop, with a view to having him
step in temporarily, later down the track, should family
circumstances force Grey to step out. Now all Grey had
to do was convince the powers that be that project sharing
with Tank was an excellent outcome for all concerned. Do
that, and the Galapagos project set-up would be as good
as he could make it.

The only thing that wasn't going his way was the small
matter of Charlotte's continued refusal to marry him.

'No,' she'd said when he'd broached the subject again.

No explanation, no tears or recriminations. Just a smiling, steadfast no.

The day of departure came around all too soon for Grey.
He'd worked every day and long into each night for almost
three weeks, planning the first Galapagos trip and co-
ordinating team members and equipment, identifying

priorities, sorting out glitches, and stamping his will on the way things would be done.

Charlotte came through in spades during this time, backburnering her own work in order to offer him the support that he'd hitherto offered her. Setting Millie—who now worked for the Greenstone Foundation—at his disposal when it came to admin tasks or tracking down certain pieces of equipment. She offered her own time when it came to prepping him for the trip and her extensive light-living and on-the-road expertise showed with every choice she made.

They ate together, laughed together, sailed together, and she slept in his arms, and on the day of Grey's departure Charlotte stood on the front steps of the house, beneath the portico, with Derek on one side of her and Millie on the other, and bade him farewell.

'You'll be calling me if you need me, day or night, it doesn't matter,' Grey told her firmly. 'I've left my mother's numbers on the fridge—home, work, and mobile. If you can't contact me, call her.'

'Absolutely.' If she was dismayed by his leaving, it didn't show.

'I *mean* it.'

'I know.' A crack, a tiny crack in her polished façade. A moment of desolation that she covered up with a bright bright smile.

'He's a little on the anxious side, isn't he?' Millie murmured.

That he was. 'And you...' Grey speared Millie with his sternest gaze. 'If something goes awry and Charlotte's not inclined to call me, *you* do it.'

'Of course,' said Millie soothingly.

'I won't be left out.'

'Not at all,' said Millie next.

'As for you,' he said to Derek—a grinning Derek whom he'd come to know and respect these past few weeks. 'You watch out for my future wife and the mother of my child. You do this from a respectable distance, you understand? Make sure she doesn't work herself too hard.'

'Not a problem,' said Derek cheerfully, and Grey scowled. It probably wouldn't do to beat the happy out of the man. Not if he wanted Derek to do his bidding while Grey was away.

Grey didn't linger long after that. He wasn't one for prolonged and tearful farewells. Neither, apparently, was Charlotte. She kissed him savouringly and told him to stay safe. She kissed him again and let the desperation creep in.

He told her he'd call her and she nodded and smiled and stepped back in place between Millie and Derek, and then he left before he changed his mind and stayed.

'Man's a goner,' said Derek.

'Well, he's gone, at any rate,' said Millie.

'He'll be back, and sooner than you think.' Derek tugged a lock of Charlotte's hastily tied ponytail and put his hands to her shoulders and turned her around to face the door.

'He's away for a month,' said Charlotte. She'd worn her favourite sundress for Greyson's departure, a high-waisted free-flowing floral silk that ended at her knees. Charlotte glowed these days, be it with happiness or with hormones. Skilful application of make-up had ensured that she glowed in particularly appealing fashion today. So that he wouldn't forget her. So that he'd think of her on his travels with pleasure and not dismay. Trying to make this farewell easy for him, and she *had* made it easy for him, hadn't she?

Over twenty years and a world's worth of practice had made perfect.

Farewells she could do.

Even when they broke her heart.

The Galapagos archipelago was everything Grey had hoped for and more. It appealed to the adventurer in him and more than satisfied the scientist. The other scientists working on the project were skilled, intrepid, and ready to work. The younger ones accepted his leadership without question because they knew how fortunate they were to be involved in the project. Some knew him and had worked with him before. The two grey-haired scientists—a biologist and an entomologist—knew the game of leadership and let him get on with it. They approved of Joey Tank's continued involvement—he won credit points with them for that. They wouldn't oppose him until something threatened their work. Grey intended to see that nothing did.

Communication was the only drawback. They had satellite phone, fax, and Internet but the service depended on the sending and receiving of strong signals, and that varied with movement. Boats moved. He sent messages to Charlotte when he could. He convinced himself it would be enough.

He found himself thinking about her at the oddest times. What she'd be doing, how the foundation was coming along. The university had really missed an opportunity to collaborate with Charlotte on that one, for the minute she'd set it up cheque books had opened and money had come pouring in. Declarations of faith in her abilities, Greyson had called them, and Charlotte had glowed, and worked twice as hard to prove herself worthy.

Charlotte wanted the foundation's first dig to be a triumph. Grey's hopes for her success were just as high. And

everything—his work and hers—would be so much easier
if only Charlotte would agree to travel.

Grey missed her. He wanted Charlotte's smiles when
he woke up in the morning and he wanted her in his bed
of a night. He wanted to watch her delighted responses
to her changing shape and he desperately wanted to see
her with his child in her arms—he didn't want to miss a
thing.

He was the man who wanted it all.

Pining for Greyson wasn't part of Charlotte's plan. Greyson
had his work and Charlotte had hers, and she made good
headway with it. She met the neighbours, took exercise
daily, ate nutritious food, and took better care of herself
than she would have had she not been pregnant.

Charlotte emailed whenever Grey did, which was surprisingly often given the erratic communication services
she knew to exist in the Galapagos. She appreciated his efforts to stay connected and smiled at the photos he emailed
through and the comments that went with them. Her baby's
father had a sense of humour. Good to know.

Day fourteen was a hard one. Loneliness stalked her
these days, no matter how hard she tried to fill the hole
Greyson had left with work. She hadn't heard from him in
three days. Nothing to worry about, but worry she did.

Fretfully.

Needlessly—because he was probably simply out of
communications range. It happened in such places. It happened a lot.

Two more days passed without word from Greyson.

Two more after that.

The emergency contact person on the card in her wallet
had always been Aurora. It needed changing and on day
nineteen of Greyson's first stint in the Galapagos Charlotte

sat down and filled out a new emergency contact card for her wallet and put, not Greyson's phone number down, but his mother's. She hadn't forgotten the importance of having someone nearby, on the ground, when things went wrong. Someone who could be there in timely fashion to pick up the pieces of a child's life and wade through all the red tape. She needed to change her will as well, but to what? Leave all her worldly possessions to her next of kin? Was it too early to do that? Too morose? This baby hadn't even been born yet. Maybe until it was, the money should go to the Greenstone Foundation. Or Greyson. Or be put in trust, to be held by Greyson. Or something.

Aurora would have known what to do. Aurora, who'd been unafraid and full of affirmation. *Never be afraid to live, Charlotte.* How many times had Charlotte heard that? *Living,* not mourning or brooding or worrying about things that would probably never come to pass.

Only every now and then they did come to pass.

A trip to the solicitor's, then, to discuss futures and fortunes and hopefully set Charlotte's mind at ease. She made the appointment for four the following afternoon and vowed to sleep better that night because of it.

Maybe Charlotte's mind was just too full or too empty on her way to the solicitor's office. Maybe that was why she didn't see that the other driver had failed to stop at the Give Way. But her mind wasn't blank when she was sitting in the smoking car with the steering wheel jammed up against her solar plexus and the door caved into her side.

Her head... She could still move her head, that was good, right? And her arms, she could move them too. Stuck, just stuck, and something just stuck could be cut out of wreckage; all it took was a little patience and time.

Breathing took effort. Charlotte had read about how

when lungs were punctured they would fill up with blood. No blood here, not much anyway, except for the stuff trickling down from her forehead. Glass cut, most likely. Glass from the shattered windscreen.

Airbags were a bitch when they'd only half opened. Airbags came with white dust and the dust was everywhere. Airbags could be punctured too. Charlotte wondered hazily how much blood *they* could fit in them.

Charlotte's mind was far from empty in the moments after the crash and before oblivion claimed her.

She had plenty of time to ponder distance and travel time and come to the conclusion that the Galapagos Isles were a very long way away. She had time to think of Greyson and to apologise for what she'd done. She had time to construct a mantra, a silent outcry of fear and of pain. Over and over the same words repeated. Over again until darkness chased them away.

My baby.

Charlotte woke in a colourless hospital room.

A hospital room was good. Meant she was still here. That she was breathing without the assistance of tubes and masks meant even better things. She closed her eyes and concentrated on her body. Moving toes: check. Fingers: likewise. Baby:

Baby.

Charlotte forced her eyes open again and spotted a woman sitting by her bedside. She knew this face. Not well. Hardly at all. But she knew it and was grateful for its presence. A doctor. An experienced one.

Greyson's mother.

'Hello, Charlotte. Are you awake?'

Olivia had her doctor's voice on, soothing yet firm.

'Yes.'

'Do you know where you are?'

'Yes.'

'Who you are?'

'Yes.' Charlotte. But not just Charlotte. 'Is my baby okay?'

'There's been some spotting.' Olivia's voice had softened and her eyes were kind. 'A little more bleeding than we'd like. An ultrasound will tell us more. You have some chest trauma. Concussion. You're very lucky not to have displaced a rib or damaged your lungs.'

But Charlotte's attention had snagged on the only thing that mattered to her. *An ultrasound will tell us more…* 'Will I lose my baby?'

'It's too early to tell,' said Olivia gently and Charlotte looked away, for the 'no' she so desperately wanted to hear had not been forthcoming. 'You haven't yet.'

'That's good, right?' she said shakily, and, with her thoughts not really in gear yet, 'Are you my doctor?'

'No, but I've seen your charts.' Olivia looked supremely uncomfortable. 'Charlotte, I'm here because you had me down as your next of kin. The hospital contacted me when they brought you in.'

'Oh.' It seemed vitally important to Charlotte to explain the why of it. 'Not *my* next of kin. Greyson's. The baby's. I didn't know who else to put down. Greyson had left your numbers on the fridge…' Not exactly the most coherent explanation Charlotte had ever given. Uncomfortable words to have to say out loud. That she had no one. That she had too often had to rely on the generosity of strangers. 'I'm so sorry. My godmother died a few months back and I have no other family. There's no one, you see… No one left.'

Olivia went silent at that. Charlotte closed her eyes and

drifted away to where the grey places beckoned. When she returned, Olivia was still there.

'I took the liberty of going through your wallet to see what kind of medical insurance you had,' said the older woman. 'They'll be shifting you up to a private wing soon. They're going to want to keep you in bed for a while. You'll be more comfortable in a private room.'

'Is my baby still with me?'

'Yes.' Conflict ran deep in Olivia's brown eyes. 'Your baby's still with you. Your chest is still a problem. There's going to be pain. Treatment for that pain is going to be complicated because of the baby.'

'I can handle the pain,' said Charlotte, and Olivia smiled wryly.

'You haven't felt it yet.'

'I haven't?' So the excruciating pressure on her chest *was* the drugged-up version? 'Oh.'

'Charlotte, I haven't been able to get hold of Greyson.'

'Doesn't surprise me.' Weak tears stung the backs of Charlotte's eyes. 'He's been out of range for about a week now.'

'I've left messages at his workplace,' Olivia said grimly. 'They're tracking him down.'

'But—Olivia, no. There's really no need to concern him with this, is there? There's nothing he can do.'

'He can be here.' The ice in Olivia's voice put Charlotte in mind of Greyson at his most formidable. Clearly he hadn't learned the fine art of intimidation from a stranger. 'For you.'

'It's just… Greyson and I…we really don't have that kind of relationship.'

Olivia stiffened. Olivia glared. Not what she wanted to hear, never mind the truth of it.

'Why don't you let him be the judge of that?'

CHAPTER NINE

RECEIVING a problem notification call from the local marine authority was never a good start to a day. Grey and his team were bunked down on the *Cantilena*, the cruiser he'd hired to get them out to the experiment sites. They were eight days gone from the main island of San Cristobal. He'd been radioing in their location every day. Government bodies had an occupational health and safety obligation to know the whereabouts of their more intrepid employees and it never hurt for other boats in the area to know where they were either.

A pan-pan call wasn't as bad as an SOS or a mayday, but good news it wasn't. Greyson made contact, they changed channels. Standard operating procedure.

'CSIRO wants *Cantilena* back in sat-phone range,' said a gruff voice, chattier now that they'd changed channels. 'Got a message in for a Dr Greyson Tyler. There's been an accident. Charlotte's in hospital. Request he phones home.'

'Say again?'

The message was the same the second time round.

'Wilco.' Will comply.

'We'll tell them you've received the message and you're coming in. Station one out.'

And that was that.

Grey put the radio handpiece back in its cradle. He ducked his head, ran his hand through his hair. Heaven help him, he was in the middle of *nowhere*, with two scientists overnighting on the island nearby and scientific equipment scattered across four atolls. Leadership weighed heavily on his shoulders, *God*, it weighed a lot, for there'd be no leaving either people or equipment behind.

He rubbed his hands down his face, and turned to find at least half of the team standing on deck, watching him in silence. No one seemed keen to break that silence.

'So,' he said finally. 'Nothing maritime, just a message for me. Charlotte's my...' His *what*, exactly? She wouldn't even marry him. 'Significant other. We live together. She's pregnant.'

Silence followed his words. Silence and no little pity.

'Did a stint as a satellite engineer in my youth,' said grey-haired Ray into that heavy waiting silence. 'I reckon if we take the sat phone off the boat and onto the island and butcher up an antenna, we might just get a signal. I reckon it's worth a try.'

Grey ran his hands through his hair again, every instinct telling him not just to phone but to *go*. Back to San Cristobal and out of there on a plane. Ecuador, Hawaii, *Sydney*. But there were other people to be considered, experiments to consider, and he'd know better what course to take once he knew more about Charlotte's situation. 'Okay,' he said to Ray gruffly. 'Okay, do it.'

Grey arrived back in Sydney forty-seven hours and thirty-six minutes after talking to his mother on the jimmy-rigged phone. He'd travelled by boat and by bus and three different types of plane and by the time he hit the ground in Sydney he felt like hell and smelled worse. Early evening, Sydney time, and Olivia stood waiting for him at the arrival gates—mothers were like that. Sadly, they were also big on hygiene—particularly mothers who were doctors and who had filthy sons who wanted to be taken straight to the hospital. Olivia told him in no uncertain terms that he'd need a shave, a shower, and possibly fumigation before he went anywhere *near* Charlotte or a hospital.

Hard not to shoot the messenger, but he managed to nod and stay calm and direct her to the Double Bay house. He used his key to get in, left his mother in the kitchen and headed for the shower. By the time he was clean, clothed, and back in the kitchen, his mother was thin of lip and steely of eye. He knew that look. He didn't have time for it.

'This is where you live?' his mother wanted to know.

'Yes.'

'Who owns it?'

'Charlotte. She owns it outright. I dare say she owns plenty of things outright. Any more questions?'

'Yes. Is this baby yours?'

'Yes, the baby's *mine*. *Charlotte's* mine.' And he needed to see her. 'Where is she? Which hospital?' His Ducati was in the garage. Not that he wasn't grateful for his mother's support, but if she was more interested in chewing him out for his irresponsible actions than in taking a drive to the hospital, he'd get there under his own steam.

'Westmead,' she said. 'And why didn't you tell me Charlotte was pregnant?'

'Charlotte was still in her first trimester when I left. She didn't want it widely known. Not yet.'

'Greyson, I'm your *mother*.'

'Noted.'

'I'm also the person on Charlotte's emergency contact card,' Olivia said curtly. 'Why aren't you?'

* * *

Mothers were levelers; at least, Grey's mother was. She'd dropped him at the hospital and continued on her way, but her question gnawed at him all the way down the long corridors until he got to the ward Charlotte was in. Not visiting hours, but his mother had pre-empted an out-of-hours visit from him and the nurses had known who he was and how far he'd come and let him through.

'See if you can convince her to take some pain medication,' said the sister on the desk. 'Even paracetamol would be better than nothing, and it won't hurt the baby.'

His mother had explained Charlotte's chest trauma—muscle tear, cracked ribs, bruising, swelling. Pain. 'Where is it?' he said. 'The medication.'

'I'll be there in a few minutes and I'll bring it with me. Room 313, and don't wake her if she's asleep. She hasn't slept since she got here.'

Charlotte wasn't asleep. She was sitting up in the bed with a pile of pillows at her back. No television on, no lights on either, and she looked like a fey little wraith in a room full of shadows, with her ebony hair loosely plaited to one side of her face and trailing down over her shoulder. Her eyes widened when she saw him, and in their pain-glazed depths he saw dismay, mingled with relief.

She dragged up a smile from somewhere. She tried to sit up a little straighter and he saw what it cost her in the lines of pain on her pale, pale face. 'You didn't have to come,' she murmured as he entered and gently shut the door.

'My choice.'

'The baby's fine.'

'Good,' he said simply.

'Could have solved a lot of problems,' she said in a heartbreakingly ragged voice. 'Could have freed you up.'

She wouldn't look at him after that. She plucked at the lightly woven hospital blanket and wouldn't look at him.

He leaned forward and put his fingers beneath her chin to tilt her head. He wanted her eyes for these next few words and he would have them. 'No,' he said quietly. 'It wouldn't have. There'd still be you.'

He watched her eyes fill with tears that spilled onto her cheeks. He had no idea what came next. She wiped them away with shaking fingers. 'I'm feeling a little fragile at the moment,' she murmured, as if it was something to be ashamed of.

'You're entitled,' he said, and pressed a gentle kiss to the corner of her mouth before closing his eyes and resting his forehead against hers. He was feeling a little ragged around the edges himself. 'The nurses say you need to take your painkillers.'

'The baby—'

'Won't be affected.' He pulled back so he could see her eyes, but the need to soothe her was just too strong. He lifted his fingers to the curve of her face and tucked a stray strand of her hair behind her ear. 'They know what they're doing, Charlotte. Take the paracetamol, even if only for a few days. Give your body a break. Get some sleep. You'll feel better for it.'

'Yes, Doctor.'

'I mean it. We need to get you sleeping, then mobile and managing your pain before we can get you out of here.'

'Easy on the dancing, action man. The bed rest is helping the baby.'

'But you can still come home and rest there.'

Charlotte nodded. 'I got Millie to arrange for a nurse to live in for a week or so, starting from when I get home. It seemed prudent. No one would worry, then, about me being there by myself. Including me.'

Grey shook his head.

'What?' she said. 'Apparently it's a very reputable nursing service. Your mother recommended it.'

His *mother* could have offered up some hospitality of her own.

'She's been marvellous,' continued Charlotte awkwardly. 'Your mother. She just came in and…took charge. Organised the room and the doctors. Arranged for a specialist to see me. Apparently he doesn't come to this hospital. He did for me. Yesterday she arrived bearing a fresh berry yoghurt smoothie, stuffed with naturopathy's finest, and sat there until I drank it. She's worse than you.'

'I've always thought so,' said Grey. Maybe his mother wasn't so unfeeling after all. Maybe his mother had assessed the situation and decided that offering to care for Charlotte while she convalesced would have made everything just a little too convenient.

For him.

The nurse came in and stayed while Charlotte took her pills. 'They'll make you sleepy,' said the nurse. 'Don't fight it. You need the rest. And probably a few less pillows.'

'Not yet,' said Charlotte hastily and the nurse regarded her with knowing eyes.

'Sleep sitting up if you have to,' said the nurse. 'But I think you'll find it easier to lie back a little more once the meds kick in.'

'Looking forward to it,' said Charlotte.

'What do you want to do with him?' asked the nurse, shooting Grey a sideways glance.

'I'm not going anywhere,' said Grey grimly. 'If that helps the decision making process any.'

'He's one of them,' murmured Charlotte.

'So I see. Wish I had one,' murmured the nurse. 'I can't give him a bed, but the chair's not so bad. He can use one of the extra blankets if he gets cold, and you can give him some pillows. I'll leave it with you.'

The nurse left, shutting the door gently behind her.

'There's a twenty-minute wait on those pillows,' said Charlotte.

'Keep your pillows,' said Grey, and settled down into the chair with his legs stretched out before him. He closed his eyes. He let out the breath he'd taken approximately fifty-five hours ago, when the VHF call to the *Cantilena* had first come in. Three days to get here. Three days was too long.

'You look tired,' she said from the bed.

'So do you.' He opened his eyes a fraction and found her watching him.

'You should go home. Get some sleep. Really. What's there to gain by staying here?'

'Peace of mind.' Exhaustion sensed an opening and began to launch an attack. Wearily he tried to resist being dragged under. 'So this is where you invented Gil.'

'Pretty much. Except that I was the one in the chair.'

'Maybe I should invent something too.'

'Like what?' she said on a yawn. 'A fiancée?'

'No, I already have a significant other, which is a term I hate, by the way. I'd much rather have a wife.'

'Good luck with that,' murmured Charlotte, and after a pause, 'So what's she like? This wife?'

'Stubborn.'

'That's what I did too.' Charlotte's voice was growing sleepier. 'Went with what I knew. So much easier on the brain.'

'She's beautiful too.'

'Imaginary folk always are. Gil was dreadfully handsome.'

'In a tough and manly way, I hope,' murmured Grey.

The events of the last few days were finally catching up with him. Exhaustion was winning. Heaviness having its way.

'Yes. Very tough and manly, and with many fine qualities.'

'Like what?'

'Oh, the usual. Honesty. Loyalty. Fidelity. Handy. Gil was very useful.'

'My wife's not so much useful as essential,' murmured Grey. 'I thought one time, about a hundred years ago, that I could use her as an anchor. That I could go off and do my thing, and come back and there she'd be, perfectly willing to pick up where we'd left off. Didn't work.'

'Why not?' Charlotte's voice was nothing more than a sleepy whisper.

'I missed her too much. Nearly went insane when I couldn't get back to her in time when she needed me. If anything had happened to her...' He had a feeling that that particular game of *what if* would have him waking up in a cold sweat for years to come.

'What would you have done?'

'Blamed myself.'

'Dumb.'

'I needed to get back to her in time, you see. To tell her how much I loved her, because I never had. Not with words. Nothing mattered except telling her that.'

'Mh.' Hard to tell if that was a word or a snore. Grey forced his eyes open and hauled himself out of the chair. He went over to the bed and slipped first one pillow from the pile behind Charlotte's back, and then another. He didn't want them for himself; he just wanted to make Charlotte more comfortable.

'What's her name?' Charlotte snuggled down into the

remaining pillows as he drew the blanket gently over her. Moments later she was asleep.

'Charlotte,' he said huskily. 'Her name's Charlotte.'

CHAPTER TEN

HAVING Greyson home and taking care of her was the sweetest form of torture. The live-in nurse had not eventuated—Greyson had eventuated, and he hovered like a protective lover and father-to-be and he kissed and held her often. Long leisurely tastes of her and quick stolen kisses, he delighted in them both and Charlotte in turn delighted in him.

They slept in the same bed but they held off with the lovemaking. Two weeks, the specialist had said. Longer, if she felt uneasy about the notion or if she had any more spotting, but there'd been no more of that.

Almost all of Greyson's Galapagos project scientists were back in Australia now. Two team members had volunteered to stay behind and hold the fort. The group would rotate the stay-behind duty, but according to Greyson there were enough willing hands up for more than one stint at being left behind that the ones who had responsibilities back home wouldn't need to ante up if they didn't want to. He was more than happy with his team. There were some fantastic, experienced, and multi-skilled people on it. All this Charlotte gleaned from a relatively communicative Greyson.

What she *hadn't* managed to glean from him was

when *he'd* be heading out next and how long he planned to be away.

Truth be told, the man seemed to be having a wee bit of trouble leaving her side. A development that amused the hell out of Millie and Derek, and even Greyson's mother, the formidable Olivia, who'd taken to dropping by a few times a week to check on Charlotte's progress.

'How does it look?' asked Charlotte some three weeks after the accident, shirt off and bra on as she sat on the edge of the long narrow hallway sideboard that Olivia had deemed suitable as a makeshift examination table. Nothing like undressing in front of one's potential mother-in-law to break down a few barriers.

'Lie back,' said Olivia briskly, and Charlotte obliged and Olivia began to press down on Charlotte's ribs, one section at a time. 'Tell me when it hurts.'

But it didn't hurt and Charlotte sat up beaming. 'That's good, right?'

'Right,' said Olivia dryly. 'But no moving mountains just yet.'

'I don't want to move mountains.' Charlotte's words came out muffled courtesy of the shirt she was tugging over her head. 'Just Greyson.'

She pulled the shirt down and eased off the sideboard to find Olivia regarding her with guarded eyes. 'Olivia, may I ask you an awkward medical question?'

'If you must.' Olivia had a pained look on her face. Olivia had probably been a doctor long enough to know where this conversation was going.

'It's just that since the accident Greyson and I haven't— I mean, we don't—and I'd like to, and it's okay to now, right? The specialist said two weeks, and it's been three, so...'

'As long as you're careful.'

'Great. Thanks.' No need to dwell on the subject. No need to go anywhere near the subject with Greyson's mother ever, *ever*, again. Fortunately, Charlotte had another question lined up, which would steer the conversation elsewhere. 'Olivia, may I ask you advice on another issue? It's not medical. It's about Greyson.'

'That boy,' said Olivia. 'What's he done now?'

'Nothing,' said Charlotte defensively. And at the glimmer of amusement in Olivia's eye, 'Oh, I get it. Mothers are allowed to criticise their children. Just…no one else can.'

'Exactly.' Olivia offered up a smile, and Charlotte blinked. 'So, what's he done? Apart from nothing.'

'I'm worried that he's neglecting his work. Because of me. He won't say when he's going back to the Galapagos. I'm worried that he'll abandon this project altogether in favour of staying here in Sydney. With me.'

'Most pregnant women I know would want their partners at their side,' commented Olivia mildly.

'I do. But not at the expense of taking away everything Greyson's worked hard for. I know what your son is, Olivia. I know what he needs and it's freedom, and challenge, and the world at his fingertips. I won't trap him. I refuse to.'

'Then go with him,' said Olivia.

'I was thinking more along the lines of staying here and encouraging Greyson to come and go. That was the pre-accident agreement. It doesn't seem to be the post-accident one.'

'I should hope not,' said Olivia sternly. 'It's about time Greyson realised that he now has responsibilities beyond himself and his work. It won't break him to honour them.'

'But what if it does?' said Charlotte, and with those

words exposed her deepest fears. 'What if turning away from the work and the lifestyle he loves does break him?'

'Or you could go with him,' said Olivia. 'Given the extensive travelling you're accustomed to, I really don't see why that's out of the question. Good medical care can be found almost everywhere these days if money is no object, and in your case it doesn't seem to be. Come back for the birth of my grandchild. Compromise.'

Charlotte ran a hand through her hair, sorting through Olivia's words and her bone-deep resistance to them. 'I stopped travelling when my godmother retired,' she said hesitantly. 'I was ready to stop. I'd been ready for years. I wanted—needed—a place to belong. A home. I still want that.'

'Charlotte, do you love my son?'

'I do.' Charlotte eased off the sideboard and together she and Olivia walked back towards the kitchen where cups of tea beckoned and confidences were encouraged. 'He's everything I've ever dreamed of in a man. And so much more.'

'That's good,' said Olivia. 'Because if I'm any judge of my son, he certainly loves you. Enough to give up his Galapagos posting and stay by your side if that's what you want, and what you need from him.'

'But it's *not* what I want.' Charlotte felt the sting of tears behind her eyes. 'I don't *know* what I want.'

'I've never told you how I met Greyson's father, have I?' said Olivia conversationally, helping herself to the tea leaves and spooning them into Aurora's old tin pot. 'I was a very earnest young doctor interning at Randwick Hospital. Seth was a skipper on a forty-metre super yacht. He'd brought a crewman who'd dislocated his shoulder into Casualty. I had dinner with him when my shift finished.

Two months later I was sailing around the world with him. Greyson was born eight months later. We married six months after that, on a beach in Tahiti. Seth wasn't skippering super yachts any more, at this point. We had another yacht, a smaller one, and we were on our way back to Australia. It took us three more years to get there.'

'Really?' Charlotte's mind boggled at the carefree picture the immaculate Olivia Greenstone had painted. 'You raised Greyson on a boat?'

'Many ports. Many boats, some of which I loved more than others.' Olivia smiled at her memories, really smiled. 'There was this one yacht…ugh. I'll tell you about it some day.'

'Tell me now,' said Charlotte, but Olivia shook her head.

'No, let me make my point first. The point being that the one truth I learned during that time we were travelling around was that as long as Seth and Greyson were with me, I could turn anywhere into a home. *Our* home. As long as they were with me.'

'But you only did three years of it,' countered Charlotte. 'It gets harder.' So much harder with the years.

'And that's something Greyson would do well to take into account,' said Olivia. 'As his father did, when he brought us home.'

'How did it end?' asked Charlotte, totally fascinated. '*Why* did it end?'

'It ended back here in Sydney,' said Olivia. 'With a job in yacht design for Seth, a little boy who needed schooling and children his own age to play with, and a chance for me to return to the medical profession. Charlotte, I know I'm biased. I want what's best for my son and always will, but you're family now and I want what's best for you too. Take a chance on Greyson. Go with him the next time he goes to the Galapagos. Maybe the time after that, he'll feel happier about leaving you here. Maybe you'll happily go with him again. Things might get chaotic for a while, given the amount of work you both have on and the imminent arrival of my grandbaby, but I'm confident that if you could just bring yourself to *trust* your instincts and Greyson's…love will lead you home.'

Charlotte stewed over Olivia's words for two long days, turning them inside out and upside down looking for flaws, or dishonesty or hidden agendas. She didn't find any. She needed to know what Greyson was thinking when it came to the Galapagos project and going away. She needed to know these thoughts sooner rather than later.

By Charlotte's reckoning, today was the day.

A sweet autumn Saturday and they were cleaning out Aurora's study; a mammoth job that involved Greyson hefting and Charlotte directing from the comfort of Aurora's leather studded office chair that lived behind a vast mahogany desk. Such blatant displays of power and wealth didn't come cheap, and Charlotte planned to put them to good use for the foundation. This would be the shakedown room, the place where *her* will met the wills of influential investors and project partners.

Just as soon as they'd cleared the last of Aurora's things away, and sorted out exactly where their combined priorities lay.

Greyson had found one of her father's journals, half an hour or so ago, and Charlotte had settled back in the fancy chair to read it. The chair reclined in armchair fashion and the table had seemed as good a place for her feet as any. Greyson had sniggered when she'd made herself at home.

'If only your archaeology students could see you now,'

he murmured, between toting and hauling and proving himself a thoroughly useful individual. 'I knew that get-up that the good Professor Greenstone wore to work wasn't the real you.'

'Wait till you see what Director Greenstone of the Greenstone Foundation has in store for you,' she promised in dulcet tones. 'She's going to be channelling Katharine Hepburn. Besides, you can talk, Mr Eminent Botanist. Where's your tweed jacket with the elbow patches?'

'I don't own one.'

'Surely, though, you own a shirt?'

He grinned in thoroughly wicked fashion before turning his back on her and hauling down yet another stack of books from the highest row of bookshelves, giving her a stunning view of tanned skin and manly back muscles at play. 'I own several shirts,' he said loftily. 'But even in the field, the wearing of one is optional.'

As far as Charlotte was concerned, this was just one more reason to go with him next time he ventured forth.

'Greyson, when are you going to the Galapagos again?'

He shot her a lightning glance and kept right on toting.

'I'm not,' he offered finally. 'I'm off the project just as soon as they find a replacement.'

'Oh.' It was worse than she'd thought. Far, far worse. 'That's a pity. I was hoping to join you there this time. I wanted to see the tortoises.'

'Tortoises,' he echoed stupidly, box of books still in hand.

'And the iguanas.'

No repetition on the iguana statement.

'And I wanted to be with you.'

'You can be,' he said gruffly. 'Here.'

'Here's overrated,' she murmured. 'Especially when it comes at so high a cost.' Time to change tack. 'There's some interesting information in this diary. Very interesting, and very useful. For example, my father talks about a promising archaeological site that he wanted to go back to some day. In Ecuador. That's near the Galapagos.'

'I know where it is, Charlotte.' Grey dumped the books on the window seat and turned to face her, one deliciously dishevelled man with don't-mess-with-me in his eyes.

'I'm just saying,' she said mildly.

'*What* are you saying?' he snapped, not so mildly. Testy. Maybe their continued lack of sexual intimacy *was* getting to him more than he let on. Something else Charlotte planned to fix before this day was through.

'I'm just saying that you can't babysit me for the rest of your life, much as it seems to be your main goal at this particular point in time. You'd go mad. *I'd* go mad. And your career would go down the drain. That's not a scenario that appeals to me. Speaking of which, you should probably email bigwig Ellie and tell her you've changed your mind about giving up the Galapagos project leadership. I'd be inclined to tell her that, give or take a month either side of our baby's due delivery date, you'll stay on the job. As for your next trip, you can drop me in Ecuador on the way. We can meet up on some little island paradise on the weekends. You could bring a shirt. Or not.'

'Drop you in Ecua—' Greyson seemed to be have difficulty keeping up his end of the conversation. 'Are you *insane*?'

'Now is that any way to speak to your future wife?'

'*What?*'

'I forgive you, of course. I'll chalk it up to you being overwhelmed by my brilliant plan. As for getting married, it seems only prudent if we're going to be travelling

together, especially with the baby. Authorities are very
fond of minors travelling with natural parents of the same
surname. It saves all sorts of lengthy explanations, and I
should know. Having a different surname from Aurora's
was the bane of our lives.'

But Greyson would not be sidetracked. 'We are *not*
travelling to Ecuador with the baby.'

'I thought you said you *wanted* a wife and family who'd
be open to travel,' argued Charlotte sweetly.

'That was before I *had* one!'

'Not that you do,' said Charlotte. 'Have one, that is.
Strictly speaking, we'd have to be married for that particular statement to hold true.' She eyed the flint-eyed piece
of steaming, stupendously muscled manhood standing
before her with a thoughtful yet fully appreciative gaze.
'What are you doing next Wednesday?'

Dr Greyson Tyler, eminent botanist, expedition leader and
all round useful guy, wasn't an unreasonable man. He
tolerated insanity in others. He took his time and tried to
work around it. He stayed calm and employed patience,
secure in the knowledge that good sense and superior
powers of reasoning would eventually hold sway. They
had to, now more so than ever. This was his future wife
and child they were talking about.

Unfortunately, all his fine qualities seemed to have
temporarily deserted him.

'What kind of man drags his wife and newborn to the
end of the earth and back?' he roared.

'So…you're opposed to the idea?' said Charlotte.

'*Yes*, I'm opposed to the idea! It's a very *bad* idea.'

'Even though I have a comprehensive knowledge of
what's involved and you have a wonderfully protective
streak that should stand us in good stead?'

Greyson glared at her.

Charlotte stifled a delighted grin. Olivia had been so right. There *was* compromise to be had here—in Greyson, and within herself. A commitment to family that would always bring them home. 'Okay,' she said. 'Let's assume that I *do* happen to agree with you when it comes to traipsing around Ecuador with a newborn. Let's assume that I want to give birth here in Sydney and get the hang of motherhood with grandparents in tow, and a doting Millie, and a long-suffering Derek, and most of all with you at my side. I'll give you that one.'

'Keep talking,' said Greyson, so she did.

'I'm talking about travelling with you to the Galapagos throughout my second trimester and maybe a little way into the third. I'm talking about finding me somewhere lovely to stay on San Cristobal, somewhere with good hospital facilities just in case, while you go do your work and Millie and Derek go looking for my father's site. I'm talking about not being emphatically opposed to travelling with you if future work opportunities demand it. We could choose our locations carefully. We could keep this as our home. We could have the best of both worlds.'

'Are you serious?'

'Very.' Time to get up and walk towards him, take his hands in hers, and make him see that when it came to their future together she was and would always be serious. 'I recently had a little epiphany.'

'That makes two of us,' he muttered.

'Mine was about belonging,' she said. 'I'd been working towards it for a while but you hastened it along, and a recent conversation with your mother simply clarified where I was headed. Having a permanent home has always been this shining dream for me, you see. Home was the place where nothing bad ever happened and I was always in control—my perfect world where parents never died and I was surrounded by a family who loved me. Thing is, that place was always just a dream. Make believe to keep the loneliness at bay. The same way Gil was make believe. None of it was ever real. You are.'

'That was your epiphany?' he said, and a smile tugged at the corners of his lips. 'That I'm real?'

'No, it's that being home isn't about staying put and living in the one place. It's about being with the man I love. Supporting him. Being there for him. And trusting him to know that when we do need to settle in one place for a time and raise our family, we will.'

'I need to think,' he muttered. 'My epiphany involved staying here because that was what you wanted. Safety. Security. Stability. You walked away from me once because I couldn't offer that to you—*wouldn't* offer it. I'm offering it to you now.'

'We *do* seem to be at cross purposes, don't we?' Charlotte sent him an encouraging smile. 'But never fear. You'll come round to my way of thinking eventually.'

But at this, he shook his head. 'I can't think here. I need to think.' He broke away from her and strode to the window, a man in need of clarity, a man at the end of his wits. 'I'm going for a swim.'

'Excellent idea,' murmured Charlotte. 'The pool's beautifully warm.' She'd already taken a dip in it to do the stretching exercises the physio had recommended for her ribs and chest. She stretched again now, drawing Greyson's gaze, deliberately adding physical desire to the cauldron and stirring gently. 'Are bathers optional?'

'Not in the pool,' he said darkly. 'In the harbour.'

'Oh.' Charlotte shuddered. 'You're on your own there.' She wasn't opposed to beach swimming or snorkelling around pristine island atolls; she loved the water.

But Sydney Harbour was different. 'Bring back some apples.'

'You have a distinct problem with reality,' he countered. 'You know that, don't you?'

'*Hello-o.*' Time to return to her chair and give her man the thinking time he'd demanded. Time to retreat behind the pages of her father's journal. 'Archaeologist.'

'Believe me, I hadn't forgotten,' he said grimly. 'Oh, and, Charlotte?'

'Hmm?' She peered over the top of the journal. 'You spoke, my love?'

'You mentioned marriage,' he said curtly.

'Yes. So I did.'

'Wednesday's fine.'

While Greyson cooled off in the water and planned his next move, Charlotte took advantage of his absence and planned hers. Sunset wasn't all that far away and one thing their bedroom did have was a spectacular viewing window to the west and a harbour view that had sold the house to Aurora in the first place.

Greyson didn't need candles but Charlotte lit some anyway. A man with a lot on his mind deserved as much. The nightgown she chose to wear was a wondrous piece of lavender silk and lace. The slave bracelets at her wrists added a nice hint of pagan. She shook out her hair and checked her ribs for tenderness. Feeling good. Still a little faded yellow bruising here and there, but the plan was to try and keep this nightgown *on* for the most part, and make Greyson forget her injuries and her recent brush with catastrophe. Life was for living, and live it she would.

Thank you, Aurora. You'd like him, I think. Greyson. My fiancé. He's useful, and honourable, and he helped me find my way home.

If wishes were wishes…
My wish has come true.

Greyson came back from the harbour all showered and shaved and tidied up. He'd cleaned up on his boat, he'd put a shirt on over the knee length canvas shorts he usually reserved for sailing. It was a very nice shirt, collared, dove grey, as soft and as warm as cotton could be—Charlotte knew this from experience. He'd even buttoned it up.

Greyson's eyes gleamed when he saw her. He looked like a man refreshed and ready for anything. Including her.

'Feel better?' she asked, and crossed to the sideboard where she'd set up a mini bar. Lime and soda for her, smooth Scotch in a round glass for him and she handed it to him with a smile and a challenge.

'Much better.'

'Decisive?'

'Very.' He eyed her nightgown with gratifying appreciation and her slave bracelets with sharp speculation. 'And how is my fiancée feeling this fine, fine evening?'

'Obliging.'

'That's good.' Greyson's voice had deepened to a husky rumble. 'That's very good.'

'I thought we might enjoy the sunset together.' Charlotte sipped her soda and admired the view before her. So much to admire about this man. The compromises he'd been willing to make for her and their child. His fierce intelligence and impressive focus. His strength of will and that beautiful hard body that he'd kept on a leash of late, on account of her injuries. She loved his protectiveness, for it spoke of his love for her. She loved *him*, body and soul. 'If you wanted to, that is.'

'I do.'

'And then I thought you might want to enjoy me.'

'I do.' Greyson set his drink aside. 'Never doubt it.'

Charlotte gently set her drink next to his. She slid her hands up to his shoulders and around the back of his neck. Greyson's lips touched hers, gentle and worshipping. Not what she wanted from this man tonight. She deepened the kiss. Greyson's kisses grew fiercer and more passionate, but his arms did not come around her to gather her close.

'The doctor said—' he began, and she shushed him with gentle fingers.

'That was three weeks ago. The doctor says I'm fine and that our baby is fine and that there's absolutely no reason why I can't be making love to you if I'm careful.'

Charlotte freed the top few buttons on his shirt and pressed her lips to his collarbone. Greyson groaned again. Hard to say whether it was in dismay.

'Charlotte, we can't,' he said huskily. 'I can't. I'm too…'

'Protective?' she said helpfully. 'Stubborn?'

'Too afraid I'll hurt you,' he muttered and brought his hands up to her face and his lips to hers for a kiss that fed her soul. 'That I'll ask for too much and you'll give it and we'll both regret it.'

'That won't happen. I love you, Greyson Tyler. I love who you are and what you do. I'm in—all the way in—but there's balance here between us too. Can't you feel it?'

'I love you,' he murmured gruffly. 'There's nothing I want more than to share my life with you. Travel with you, stay here and raise a family with you, build a foundation, work on my own projects. I want it all.'

'I'm glad to hear it. Because I want it all too, including your lovemaking.' Charlotte stepped away from his touch, put her hand in his, and led him to the bed, urging him onto it, on his back, exactly where she wanted him. 'Starting from now.' She straddled him carefully, clothes and all. Plenty of time for the removal of clothes later. 'We can do this.' Leaning forward, she set her hands to Greyson's shoulders and watched with satisfaction as his eyes flared and darkened. 'We *are* doing this.' She kissed the edge of his lips and the line of his jaw until finally she reached his ear.

'What's more,' she whispered, 'we're going to love it.'

Harlequin *Presents*

Coming Next Month

from **Harlequin Presents®**. Available June 28, 2011.

Coming Next Month

from **Harlequin Presents® EXTRA**. Available July 12, 2011.

Visit www.HarlequinInsideRomance.com
for more information on upcoming titles!

REQUEST YOUR FREE BOOKS!

Harlequin *Presents*®

PASSION GUARANTEED SEDUCTION

2 FREE NOVELS PLUS
2 FREE GIFTS!

YES! Please send me 2 FREE Harlequin Presents® novels and my 2 FREE gifts (gifts are worth about $10). After receiving them, if I don't wish to receive any more books, I can return the shipping statement marked "cancel." If I don't cancel, I will receive 6 brand-new novels every month and be billed just $4.05 per book in the U.S. or $4.74 per book in Canada. That's a saving of at least 15% off the cover price! It's quite a bargain! Shipping and handling is just 50¢ per book in the U.S. and 75¢ per book in Canada.* I understand that accepting the 2 free books and gifts places me under no obligation to buy anything. I can always return a shipment and cancel at any time. Even if I never buy another book, the two free books and gifts are mine to keep forever.

106/306 HDN FC55

Name _____ (PLEASE PRINT) _____

Address _____ Apt. # _____

City _____ State/Prov. _____ Zip/Postal Code _____

Signature (if under 18, a parent or guardian must sign)

Mail to the **Reader Service:**
IN U.S.A.: P.O. Box 1867, Buffalo, NY 14240-1867
IN CANADA: P.O. Box 609, Fort Erie, Ontario L2A 5X3

Not valid for current subscribers to Harlequin Presents books.

**Are you a current subscriber to Harlequin Presents books
and want to receive the larger-print edition?
Call 1-800-873-8635 or visit www.ReaderService.com.**

* Terms and prices subject to change without notice. Prices do not include applicable taxes. Sales tax applicable in N.Y. Canadian residents will be charged applicable taxes. Offer not valid in Quebec. This offer is limited to one order per household. All orders subject to credit approval. Credit or debit balances in a customer's account(s) may be offset by any other outstanding balance owed by or to the customer. Please allow 4 to 6 weeks for delivery. Offer available while quantities last.

Your Privacy—The Reader Service is committed to protecting your privacy. Our Privacy Policy is available online at www.ReaderService.com or upon request from the Reader Service.

We make a portion of our mailing list available to reputable third parties that offer products we believe may interest you. If you prefer that we not exchange your name with third parties, or if you wish to clarify or modify your communication preferences, please visit us at www.ReaderService.com/consumerschoice or write to us at Reader Service Preference Service, P.O. Box 9062, Buffalo, NY 14269. Include your complete name and address.

USA TODAY *bestselling author B.J. Daniels*
takes you on a trip to Whitehorse, Montana,
and the Chisholm Cattle Company.

RUSTLED

Available July 2011 from Harlequin Intrigue.

As the dust settled, Dawson got his first good look at the
rustler. A pair of big Montana sky-blue eyes glared up at
him from a face framed by blond curls.

A woman rustler?

"You have to let me go," she hollered as the roar of the
stampeding cattle died off in the distance.

"So you can finish stealing my cattle? I don't think so."
Dawson jerked the woman to her feet.

She reached for the gun strapped to her hip hidden under
her long barn jacket.

He grabbed the weapon before she could, his eyes nar-
rowing as he assessed her. "How many others are there?"
he demanded, grabbing a fistful of her jacket. "I think you'd
better start talking before I tear into you."

She tried to fight him off, but he was on to her tricks and
pinned her to the ground. He was suddenly aware of the soft
curves beneath the jean jacket she wore under her coat.

"You have to listen to me." She ground out the words
from between her gritted teeth. "You have to let me go. If
you don't they will come back for me and they will kill
you. There are too many of them for you to fight off alone.
You won't stand a chance and I don't want your blood on
my hands."

"I'm touched by your concern for me. Especially after
you just tried to pull a gun on me."

"I wasn't going to shoot you."

Dawson hauled her to her feet and walked her the rest of the way to his horse. Reaching into his saddlebag, he pulled out a length of rope.

"You can't tie me up."

He pulled her hands behind her back and began to tie her wrists together.

"If you let me go, I can keep them from coming back," she said. "You have my word." She let out an unladylike curse. "I'm just trying to save your sorry neck."

"And I'm just going after my cattle."

"Don't you mean your boss's cattle?"

"Those cattle are mine."

"*You're* a Chisholm?"

"Dawson Chisholm. And you are…?"

"Everyone calls me Jinx."

He chuckled. "I can see why."

Bronco busting, falling in love…it's all in a day's work.
Look for the rest of their story in

RUSTLED

Available July 2011 from Harlequin Intrigue
wherever books are sold.

Love Inspired

After her fiancé calls off their wedding, Brooke Clayton has nowhere to go but home. Turns out the wealthy businessman next door, handsome single father Gabe Wesson, needs a nanny for his toddler—and Brooke needs a job. But Gabe sees Brooke as a reminder of the young wife he lost. Given their pasts, do they dare hope to fit together as a family…forever?

The Nanny's Homecoming
by Linda Goodnight

◆ ROCKY MOUNTAIN HEIRS ◆

Available July wherever books are sold.

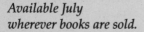

www.LoveInspiredBooks.com

LI87680